My Angelica

OTHER YEARLING BOOKS YOU WILL ENJOY:

IF I FORGET, YOU REMEMBER, *Carol Lynch Williams*
THE TRUE COLORS OF CAITLYNNE JACKSON, *Carol Lynch Williams*
THE LOTTIE PROJECT, *Jacqueline Wilson*
DOUBLE ACT, *Jacqueline Wilson*
PLANNING THE IMPOSSIBLE, *Mavis Jukes*
PIG AND THE SHRINK, *Pamela Todd*
CINDERELLA 2000: LOOKING BACK, *Mavis Jukes*
HOLES, *Louis Sachar*
FROZEN SUMMER, *Mary Jane Auch*
SAMMY KEYES AND THE CURSE OF MOUSTACHE MARY
Wendelin Van Draanen

YEARLING BOOKS are designed especially to entertain and enlighten young people. Patricia Reilly Giff, consultant to this series, received her bachelor's degree from Marymount College and a master's degree in history from St. John's University. She holds a Professional Diploma in Reading and a Doctorate of Humane Letters from Hofstra University. She was a teacher and reading consultant for many years, and is the author of numerous books for young readers.

My Angelica

Carol Lynch Williams

A YEARLING BOOK

Published by
DELL YEARLING
an imprint of
Random House Children's Books
a division of Random House, Inc.
1540 Broadway
New York, New York 10036

Visit us on the Web! www.randomhouse.com/kids
Educators and librarians, for a variety of teaching tools, visit us at www.randomhouse.com/teachers

ISBN: 0-440-22778-X

Reprinted by arrangement with Delacorte Press

Printed in the United States of America

April 2001

10   9   8   7   6   5   4   3   2

OPM

*To the writers' group
on Walton's Mountain,
who couldn't believe
those first few lines*

My
Angelica

1

Sage

"OKAY, GEORGE," I SAID. "LISTEN TO THIS."

"Another beginning, Sage?" George asked me. We sat at a table outside the Schoolcraft High School cafeteria. People milled around, calling hello, eating, laughing together. The smell of lunchroom food, tacos and hamburgers and school-made rolls, rode an autumn breeze over to where we were. Cheri walked by with her new boyfriend and waved. I waved back, then turned to George.

I nodded and smiled at him. "Another beginning," I said.

George sighed. "Go ahead."

I took a big breath and began to read my latest creation.

"Let me be frank," Angelica quipped, brushing her blacker-than-the-night hair out of her brighter-than-a-blue-sky eyes. The throng of press reporters looked at the tall, pug-nosed woman with the longing of a cow on a range of fresh grass. She twisted her silky/shiny hair around one perfectly polished finger and then pointed with a jab to the group of men. They all gasped together, at the very same

moment, a chorus of gaspers. The sound was almost snake-like.

One stood out among the crowd. Angelica felt her heart drawn out of her body against her will. She gasped, too. But her gasp was a feminine one. He was tall, young, and handsome. His bad brown eye wore a dark eye patch. His good brown eye rolled up and down, up and down, following Angelica's every movement. A television camera perched on his shoulder like a black and silver parrot. For a moment Angelica was stunned to silence, watching the one-eyed cameraman. Then she found her voice and continued eloquently, richly and deeply, like maple syrup straight from the brown bottle of Aunt Jemima:

"The story of the Franklin murders I am going to tell you is completely true," Angelica exploded. The one-eyed cameraman smiled, stretching his lips as thin as a slice of pepperoni when you look at it from the side. "I have the photos and notes to prove my findings." She waved the thick stack of papers lightly about her head. "A reporter has a duty to always tell the truth, no matter how difficult." Angelica felt her voice tighten like a rubber band pulled from one hundred miles away. It had been just over a year. It seemed so long ago and yet, and yet, so close.

"This case has been especially hard for me. Because . . ." Angelica drew herself up tall and slender like a giraffe. "Because Mr. Franklin was my beloved husband." Angelica put on her dead husband's favorite white gloves, and wiped a lone tear from her carefully made-up face. Not a bit of makeup smeared. She was exquisite in her pain. Her deep, deep, deep pain. "Because I always tell the truth," Angelica Franklin breathed frankly, "I am the best in the journalistic field. And I am always frank. I am known as the frank Franklin."

2

Angelica could tell the one-eyed cameraman had not shaved in exactly three days. No more, no less. His whiskers had a gentle way about them. Gentle yet firm. She wanted to leap into his wallet and find out his name. It took all of her willpower to turn away and begin the slide presentation that would surely change the world.

I peered over the top of my wrinkled papers and bit my lip.

George stared at me. His mouth hung open a little. I wondered how long it would be before he was shaving every day. I could see him with a face full of dark whiskers. The lone reporter to sweep Angelica off her feet. No, to sweep me off *my* feet.

"That's it?" he asked.

I smiled and nodded, feeling a slow blush creep onto my cheeks. Angelica is my hero. I want to be just like her.

"*That* took you three days to write?"

I nodded again. For a moment I *was* Angelica's twin. I, like she, could take the criticisms of my admirers. Leaning toward George, I imagined him in an eye patch.

"Sage, you told me you were creating a masterpiece for the last three days and that's why we couldn't get together to study for the ACT. It's not that much longer before we're going to be taking that test."

"Two years," I said, nodding again. I leaned a little closer to George. I could smell his clean skin.

George blinked a long blink. "Two years what?" he asked after a moment.

"Before we graduate from high school."

"One can't be too prepared," George said. His voice

was soft, and it cracked. I love it when that happens. It seems to promise a full beard and a possible eye patch. And George can never be too prepared. He's not made that way.

"So?" I asked.

"So?" George asked back.

I smiled. Ever since writing this chapter of Angelica's adventures, I've been practicing smiles in the mirror. Celebrity smiles. "What about my book? What did you think?"

George took off his glasses and polished them with great care. They were shiny already, but he polished them anyway because, I knew, he didn't know how to tell me what was on his mind. My story was just too wonderful.

"Oh, Sage," he said, and I could tell by his voice that his soul was touched by my writing. I gave him a practiced smile, my best yet, I was sure.

"Be honest with me." And how could he not be, with this magnificent piece of literature still hanging in the sound waves around us?

"The truth hurts," George said.

"That's what your mom says. She's been saying it for years."

George nodded. "And I think she's right in this case."

"What do you mean by that?" George's mom is a designer. You know—she makes other people's houses look nice. She's way into honesty. I'm not sure how designing floral wreaths and fancy curtains goes along with honesty, but Mrs. Blandford seems to think they walk hand in hand. She's always saying that "truth hurts" thing to George.

4

"It's crap, Sage."

A *C* word! I felt all the color drain from my face. "What? George, what do you mean by that?" I put my hand to my throat in a very Angelica-like way and gasped in a bit of air.

George fumbled around for something to say. "It needs work here and there, I mean."

I swallowed at a lump that was interfering with my breathing. "Where, George? I can take suggestions." I riffled the two pages like there were more.

"The whole thing. The whole thing is bad, Sage. It doesn't make sense. Maybe a few classes in creative writing would help you. We could take them together. Next year. Or maybe we could see what this little book has to say about creative writing." George patted the thick manual he'd ordered from the bookstore. *How to Study for the ACT* seemed a part of my waking nightmare. George always tells me how important college is. I don't agree with him. I'm gifted.

"I tell you, George," I said, chewing on the end of my pencil, something my father, the dentist, is always telling me not to do. "I am *not* going to college. I plan to be a writer. A successful writer. A mystery . . . or . . . or romance writer. I'll thrill the world with the beautiful Angelica." I decided not to mention the *C* word again. Maybe if I didn't, George would forget that crap comment. And the truth stuff, too.

George lifted one eyebrow. He always does that when I talk about romance. "Ms. Chapin says—"

I interrupted him. "First of all, I had plenty of similes. . . ."

"You're right."

"Secondly, you don't have to experience something to

write about it. And for all you know, Mr. George Blandford, I *have* been experiencing romance." I stared off into the distance. It wouldn't be that many more days before the snow fell. Flat white clouds skimmed across the deep blue of the early-afternoon sky. It would make a perfect setting for an Angelica story. Perhaps I could write a mystery-romance. I felt a little breathless at the thought.

"You're fifteen, Sage. You've never been kissed. Except in the second grade. You know nothing of Romance."

When George said *Romance,* it sounded like it had a capital *R.*

"I know how old I am," I said. "And anyway, I've been doing research."

"Research?" George asked.

"Yes, research. I've been talking to Cheri about kissing. She's told me all I need to know."

"Cheri is definitely the kiss encyclopedia of Schoolcraft High School," George said under his breath. Cheri and George aren't the best of friends, even though she and I are close.

I rolled my eyes. "I've never let you kiss me, but that doesn't mean I've never been kissed. Besides, I'm saving myself for the right man," I said. "And for your information, that did *not* happen in the second grade. That was a figment of your oversexed imagination."

George *is* the right man, but I haven't told him yet. I don't believe in throwing myself at anyone, much less at the one I love. It's just not very Angelica-like.

"Oversexed?" George's voice went all high and squeaky. He stared at me through his polished glasses.

"Do you let that Taylor guy kiss you? You've dated him a lot. What do you see in him anyway? He is such a jerk. There's something about that guy I do not like." An unhappy look crossed over George's face. Why, if he had an eye patch on right now, he could play the part of the one-eyed cameraman—once my book is made into a miniseries.

"You don't like anyone I go out with," I said. "You think every guy I have ever dated is a jerk."

"That's not true," George said. "I'm not a jerk." He pressed his hand against his dark green sweatshirt. "And I didn't mind so much when you went out with my cousin Jeffrey. I don't think he's a jerk." George smiled at me in a cameraman-like way, then leaned closer. Our heads almost touched. We were seconds away from our first kiss. "You've got a blue ink mark by your nose," he said.

"That's because I've been working so hard writing." I felt around my face until George finally touched the spot where I had written on myself. His fingertip was cool. I tried to rub the ink off with spit and moved away a little. No need to learn about kissing firsthand right here in front of the lunchroom. How *un*romantic. "By the way, the reason you didn't think Jeffrey was a jerk, even though he was, was because you knew he was going back to Florida and he wouldn't be around but for that one week. Not like Bob, or any of the other guys I've dated."

"Jeffrey—a jerk? Why? What did he do that was so jerky?" George didn't say anything for a moment. "He tried to kiss you, right? He told me he thought you were beautiful but he wouldn't try anything with you."

I sat quiet.

"That jerk!" George said. He pounded his fist on the ACT study guide.

"Oh, George," I said, and laughed.

George is passionate. And a perfectionist. He's already made plans to go to Kalamazoo Valley Community College, our local school, graduate with honors, then head off to Northern Michigan University at Marquette for his doctorate in English and communications. He's known this since the second grade when he and I first met. And since that day I've known that I'll be going with my passionate perfectionist.

I'll support him with my writing.

2

George

SAGE AND I HAVE BEEN BEST FRIENDS since the second grade. We probably would have started palling around in the first grade, but I lived in Washington then and she was here in Michigan, which is where my family moved not too long after I turned seven.

I remember meeting her. It was the third day of the first week of school. The kids were playing Girls Chase the Boys. I hated the game. I mean, what seven-year-old boy wants to be kissed by a girl? I wanted to read. So I hid in a low-limbed tree, with a book tucked under my arm. I still remember the title: *Prince Caspian.* I kept one eye out for anyone who might try to attack me. I had just made myself comfortable when I heard someone from above say, "Get out of this tree and run or I will kiss you right here and now." I recognized the someone as Sage, the girl who sat in the front of the class and talked a lot. She was good in math, even then.

"I said, climb on down," Sage ordered, and I did. There was no place to run in that tree. When I stood on the ground, she leaped from a limb and landed in a crouch in front of me. Then she straightened up and put her hands on her hips. I could see that she meant business.

"I'll give you one chance to get away," she said, "a head start." Before I could even move, she kissed me right on the mouth, then ran off screaming, "George Blandford is my slave for the day." I wiped her wet kiss off my lips with the back of my hand and glanced around to see who might have seen this humiliating event. No one had.

Sometimes I wonder if that kiss was the turning point in our lives. In my life. I mean, I'm your average-looking guy. I have astigmatism and can't afford to get contacts for this problem. I have a cowlick that sticks up regardless of how much mousse or hair spray I use. I've even tried Vaseline. Nothing works. I'm of average height (five-nine), have average hair color (light brown), average eye color (dark brown). I like sports, but I'm not that great at any of them. And my family is middle class. Pretty average, right?

And yet, Sage Oliver is my best friend.

And, to me, Sage is not average. To me, she's perfect. And beautiful. If I could explain a deep sigh of satisfaction, that would be Sage. She's tiny (five-two), has long strawberry-blond hair (wild-and-crazy, curly hair), straight white teeth, with no under- or overbite (her father is a dentist). And she has green, green eyes. It's through those eyes that she sees the whole world as it really isn't. As a romance novel. With Angelica as the hero. Maybe she gets this writing idea from her mother. You've probably heard of Sage's mother: Lorna Lovelocks. That's her pen name. She's quite a famous writer.

Sage is really good in math, and yet all she wants to do is write.

I've tried to help her. I've told her to stick to equations. "I've no passion for equations," she says.

I've tried to get her to sign up for Math Club.

"Math Club? Oh, George. How can I do math when

Angelica is crying out to be freed from the prison of my brain?"

I've even tried to get her to write for the school paper. But Sage thinks it's too small.

"George," she says to me every time I ask her to write something simple, like a class evaluation or a play review. "That's too easy. I need something to tax my imagination."

Wow, I thought, watching her and barely listening the last time we talked about this. We were between classes, standing around, and I was watching her every move. I felt kind of tingly. But I didn't let it show. I couldn't. Everyone knows best friends don't become serious. I think there's some unwritten rule that says best friends always stay best friends and that's it.

"It is easy writing, but, Sage, it would give you the chance you need to practice."

"Practice?" Sage's voice was dramatic. "Practice what?"

"Your writing. Or have you considered the stage?" I wasn't kidding about the stage part. Sage always acts dramatic.

"I don't need *practice,* George," Sage said, ignoring my acting comment. "I write all the time."

This is true. "That's true. But you never finish anything. And anyway, there are rules people have to follow to work with the paper. And deadlines to meet."

Sage let out a big breath. It smelled spearmint-y. "I have a perfect example of meeting deadlines, George. My mother does it all the time. She always worries about her editor or agent being unhappy."

Sage walked away that day, sure she didn't need help. I watched her go, my heart pumping so hard, I was sure someone was going to have to call the paramedics to revive me. She has a very serious walk.

It was some time later that things began to change for me. And since I wasn't expecting the change, everything seemed to start to fall apart. I knew the rule: *Best friends stay best friends no matter what.* And I had planned on living by that decree.

So I couldn't know a month or so later, when I came out into the hall from the newsroom, all that was going to happen. Who could?

I was trying to stretch out my neck. It hurt from working on the computer so long. And then I saw Sage, pushing through the crowds. Cheri was talking with her, and they both looked serious. I think the most important thing in Cheri's life is when she breaks a nail. Anyway, Sage and Cheri separated at the lockers, and Sage started toward me.

I watched her. Watched and held my breath, waiting for her to see me. It almost hurt, that waiting for her to look in my direction. And when she did, she smiled. Can I even begin to tell you what Sage's smiles do to my heart?

Trying to tame her hair with one hand and finally giving up, she came over to where I stood blocking the newsroom door. I almost forgot to breathe.

"Move it, Blandford," said Sarah Newhouse, one of the sportswriters for the paper. She shoved her way past me when I didn't step aside. It's not like I didn't want to get out of Sarah's way. Everybody gets out of her way when she says to move.

But the change had begun. The unspoken rule was now at risk. And it was all from seeing Sage. She paralyzed me.

Has that ever happened to you? Have you ever seen someone and found that you were frozen to the spot, knowing you'd remember that time and place forever? That's what had happened to me.

Sage had on a white shirt with ruffles all over it, tucked into a long denim skirt that touched the tops of her leather boots. She looked like a girl from a fantasyland, her hair streaming over her shoulders, her skin lightly tanned. I was captivated by her.

And then I wanted to do the impossible.

I wanted to break out in song, when I saw her coming toward me, walking through shafts of light that poured through the high windows and caught dust particles, then transformed them into tiny suns. I wanted to dedicate the SHS yearbook to her, even though I have absolutely no affiliation with it. I wanted to write a column about her, including thoughts and wonderings from my oversexed imagination. I wanted to write her a note and send it, folded like an airplane, on a draft of air that would land the plane right in her hand.

Dear Sage,
I love you. Do you love me? Check one box.
☐YES or ☐NO.

Yours forever,
George

With all these things rolling around in my mind, how could I catch even a glimpse of what lay ahead for the two of us?

the tree introduced us
that warm September
and we are like it now

the way the roots
nourish the brown body and strong arms and crown
of green

your smile replenishes me
toward growth

4

Sage

"I'VE GOT ANOTHER ONE," I SAID TO GEORGE. I brushed spilled popcorn from my lap to the littered floor of the theater. Lucky for me I hadn't ordered the buttered kind.

George pretended to be engrossed in the previews. I tapped on my manuscript and said, "A new start here, George."

He moved forward, staring at the screen. I could see the bright lights of an action film exploding in the reflection of his glasses.

I leaned nearer. Without waiting for his answer, I put my lips close to his ear and began to read.

The mist hung heavily over the water, thick with the smell of fish and whiskey. Angelica stood on the dock in her alligator pumps. Her blue sequined dress reflected the patterns of the Milky Way to a T. Her auburn tresses hung loose and straight down her slender back. Her dark brown eyes flashed with intensity.

The smell of death tickled Angelica's sensitive nose. On the night of her nomination for the Democratic candidacy to be the first female president of the United States of America, on the night her lover of thirteen months proposed marriage, Angelica smelled a murder mystery brewing like Folgers Coffee Crystals.

This time she would be ready for it.

Pulling herself up to her highest height, Angelica remembered her life as a battered child. She had beaten the odds like her wicked stepfather had beaten her. She wiped a lone tear from her cheek with her gloved hand.

A fisherman cast into the dark, still waters, eyeing Angelica from his casual sitting position. He wore a black eye patch. It covered one very brown eye.

George didn't move. He didn't say anything, either. Around us Dolby sounds rocked the air. I had the sudden urge to kiss George right under his ear. I pulled away from him.

George looked me in the eyes, and we both swallowed.

"Let me read it to you again," I said quickly, trying to get my mind off George's neck. "Only this time I won't whisper."

"No," George said, swallowing again. "The movie's starting now. And it's embarrassing to me whenever you turn on that penlight. People keep looking at us."

George needs to get used to people looking at us. I'm going to be famous someday, and people will always be looking at us. And asking for my autograph. It won't be that long before people are staring right at us and asking if I'm not the writer of the famous Angelica series. And George will be proud to be seen with me. I'll probably kiss his neck all the time then.

I took a handful of popcorn from the bucket on George's lap. He'd taken it from me when I'd spilled it. He's always saving me when I do something clumsy.

"So tell me what you thought," I whispered in a medium-loud voice to George. "Great beginning, isn't it? Were you captured by the mystery and romance of the whole neck?"

"Neck?" George asked.

"Sorry," I said. "I meant *thing*. Were you captured by the mystery of the whole thing?" I let out a sigh. "Couldn't you just see Angelica standing there on the rotting dock, the moon reflecting in the water?" *I* was the one standing on the dock. *I* wore the tight, blue sequined dress. And George was the one-eyed fisherman. With a very nice neck.

When he didn't answer right away, I shined the penlight into his face.

"Sage, put that down," he said, pushing the flashlight away. His hand was warm on my wrist. I clicked off the light and imagined calluses on his palms caused by a fishing pole. I could almost smell the salt air.

"Tell me what you thought, George. It really is important to me."

"It needs work."

"Where? What?"

"Well, for example, she smelled either fish, whiskey, or death. Let her pick one and concentrate on it."

"She has a sensitive nose."

"You pointed that out."

"Is that all? Other than her smeller, is there anything you'd like to say about the opening scene?"

"Your writing stinks."

"Let's not say anything about smelling at all, George," I said.

"I just want you to know that wasn't a pun," George said.

"Oh." I take everything George says with a grain of salt. Most of the time. I think George is a big teaser when it comes to my writing. And I save everything that I have ever written, whether he likes it or not. I have 638 beginnings about Angelica. I'm sure it won't be long before one of them will sweep America off its feet.

"I bet a few college classes would steer you toward the writing career you want. College is a good place to be," George said. The other *C* word. First *crap,* now *college.* "Maybe you should be thinking about which school can offer you something in the mathematics area."

"Pooh," I said.

"Pooh?" George asked.

"Yes, pooh." *Pooh* is one of the words I've been experimenting with in my Angelica beginnings. "Math is not the same as writing, George. Math is easy and, well, boring. Writing is what I love to do."

"Pooh?" George asked again.

After he gets his doctorate, George and I will settle down in a little university town and have three children. A boy first and then twin girls. I will be a well-known writer. Perhaps historical fiction will be my forte.

I kept my penlight handy, in case I was hit by any inspiration. When you're a writer, you must always be prepared for when the creating mood will strike. Also, that way I could check out George's neck whenever I felt like it.

And I did, five times.

5
George

"HAND ME A THUMBTACK," I SAID.

Sage and I walked around the school putting up posters for the annual writing contest. It was during our lunch break, and we hurried, posting advertisements on office windows, bathroom doors, and occasionally a bulletin board. Sage was eating an apple.

"What does the first-prize winner get this year?" she asked.

"Let's see." I paused long enough to remember what I had put in the paper the day before. Then in my radio announcer voice I said, "The big winner will receive the following prizes: His or her picture in the school newspaper; a review of his or her work in *The Kalamazoo Gazette;* dinner for two at T.G.I. Friday's in Portage; and, of course, he or she will read a chapter over the intercom at the beginning of each day until the work is completed, however long or short it may be."

I stabbed a thumbtack into the bulletin board in the library, then stood back and admired the poster. I was proud that Andrew, a friend of mine, and I had come up with the idea to advertise the contest this year. Usually it's announced only in English classes.

Sage and I left the library, me carrying a stack of bright yellow and purple posters (our school colors) and Sage with a box of thumbtacks and half an apple.

I was still thinking about the contest and how good Sage smelled standing right there next to me, kind of apple-y, when Cheri came up. Some guy I didn't know tagged along behind her. They were connected at the hands. I wondered how long this boyfriend would last.

"Sage," Cheri called. She waved with her free hand and clumped over to us. The guy smiled, but not at Sage and me. He couldn't seem to take his eyes off Cheri. Maybe it was her clothes.

Cheri is what Sage would call an individual. She keeps her hair cut short, she's pierced her ears a million times, and she always wears hiking boots, no matter what else she has on. It was the boots making her clump.

"Look at this," Sage said, grabbing a poster from the pile I held and taking it over to her friend. "The writing contest."

"No way," Cheri said, lifting her hands, including the one her newest friend held, to her lips. "A writing contest? A writing contest!" Cheri's voice was nearly a shriek of excitement.

Sage nodded.

"Happens every year," I said.

"Are you gunna?" Cheri asked.

"No way," Sage said.

Gunna, I thought. *Gunna?*

"George, tell her to," Cheri said. "You're the man with all the writing talent. Tell her to."

"To what?" I asked.

"To enter the contest," Cheri said. Then she looked at

the wall clock. "We're late, Randy," she said to her friend. And then to us, "We've got to get to study period. You know, make-out hour."

"Oh," I said, and the rest of my words stuck in my throat.

"Bye, you two." Cheri clumped off, pulling Randy behind her.

Sage looked at me. Her eyes shone. I could see she wanted me to tell her to enter the contest. I moved away to tack up another poster. My hands were sweating. I hoped my deodorant would hold out.

Sage came up behind me, the heels of her shoes tapping against the tile floor.

Help me, I prayed to the gods of writing. *Get me out of this.*

"I hope your stupid friend, Andrew, doesn't win again," Sage said. She stood next to me, finishing off her apple. She kind of gestured with her head at Andrew, who came toward us, carrying his own stack of posters.

"Darby," I called to him, hoping to create enough of a distraction that Sage would forget about getting me to tell her to enter the contest. "I told you I had this side of the school."

Cheri and Randy hurried past Andrew, who watched them leave, shaking his head.

"Just checking to see if you needed any help," Darby said. "I can see that you don't."

Andrew Darby is one of my best friends—not including Sage, I mean. Last year he won this very contest with a book of satirical essays.

"No, Andrew, *I'm* helping George," Sage said. She sounded a little snotty. She really doesn't like him, though

I'm not sure why. "We've got everything under control over here."

Darby said something we couldn't hear, then stomped out of sight, probably to his side of the school.

We started down the hall, looking for another place to hang a poster. Sage tossed her apple core into a garbage can as we walked past.

"Remember when he won the contest last year?" Sage asked. She didn't give me any time to answer. "Wasn't his stuff awful? I cringed with embarrassment for him every time he read anything." She shook her head, remembering. Her long hair gently waved around her face. For a minute I felt sorry for Andrew Darby. I couldn't stand it if Sage hated me. "Somebody who can really write needs to enter this year. Why don't you, George?"

I smiled at Sage. "Andrew's stuff was good," I said. Maybe this *was* an answer to my prayers. If I could get Sage's mind off the contest . . .

"No it wasn't. It was too sad. People don't like to read sad stuff."

Not only is Sage not a very good writer, she tends to only like what she calls happy writing. In other words, love spiced up with unrealistic adventure and an occasional kiss. She thinks true life is sad enough and bad enough without having to read about all the sadness and badness. There was no way she would have liked Andrew's essays about being old and saving nearly extinct animals and helping the homeless. Plus, Sage hasn't liked Andrew Darby since the moment she laid eyes on him. And vice versa. You might say Cheri and I feel the same way about each other.

"I'm not entering," I said. "I don't like competition." That's the truth. We were at another poster-placing location. I glanced at Sage. She looked at me expectantly. Oh, no. She *hadn't* forgotten that she wanted me to encourage her.

I swallowed a glob of spit. Then I told her what she wanted to hear. I had to. Say it, I mean. I felt like a puppet of love, doing something I really didn't want to do, but feeling the need to make Sage happy with my words. "You do it, instead, Sage. You enter." My mouth hardly moved.

Sage bit at her bottom lip, like she was trying not to smile. "You think so, George?"

I shrugged. "Sure, why not?"

No! I wanted to scream. *I don't think so. What I really think is that you should burn Angelica at the stake.* Now I had one more reason not to like Cheri. Could things get any worse?

Then a thought surfaced. Sage never finished any of her writing. What made me think she would finish something now? A bit of peace entered my harrowed soul. I turned to Sage and looked at her. I mean, really looked at her, past her beautiful hair and perfect skin and green, green eyes. She looked way interested in what I had just said. I started feeling nervous again.

Something clogged up my throat. I think it was my tongue.

"Maybe you could turn in something math-y," I said. It sounded like I was gargling with a bunch of numbers.

"Well, I don't know if I will enter," Sage said. She had a faraway look in her eyes. "Maybe not." She shook her head. "I don't think so."

Thank you, thank you, thank you. Relief flooded my body, making me feel light-headed. It was while I was in this light-headed state that I saw Bob Taylor, coming in at the end of the corridor. I turned my back, hoping that somehow he wouldn't recognize Sage and me. But how could he miss us?

"Hey." Bob's voice traveled down the hall. I felt my back stiffen. Sage turned toward him.

"Oh, hi," she said. Her voice sounded absolutely perfect. And it looked to me like she was absolutely happy to see him. Things had just gotten worse.

Bob came up to Sage, and I watched him out of the corner of my eye. Never in the history of our school had putting up a poster been done with greater care than it was right then—and without me looking at what I was doing.

"Sage, Sage, Sage," Bob said, and he held his hand out to her like he was holding a prize or something. "Are you busy this Friday night?"

I felt my face grow warm from anger. Couldn't he see me standing there?

"There's a party at Laverne Havenga's house, and I would be honored if you would go with me." Bob's voice changed to a weak English imitation.

I pushed the tack deep into the wood. The janitor would need a crowbar to get it out now.

"Well, Bob, let me think," Sage said. She touched my arm. "Are we doing anything this Friday night, George?"

"What?" I asked, surprised by the question. I had been listening in on the conversation, not expecting to be a part of it. I was caught off guard.

Bob Taylor laughed, and for a brief moment I hated his guts more than ever. I would have glared at him, but I was pretending not to listen.

"Are we doing anything on Friday night?" Her hand was warm on my arm.

Why in the world was she asking me? We always decided together what our weekends would be like, but not in front of other people. Usually it was a casual thing like "Let's go to the movies" or "You wanna go ice-skating?" Never this. Never the third degree with a hated enemy watching.

I kept pretending not to listen, but now I felt stupid. "Hmmm?" I answered.

She smiled at me. "Friday?"

"No, no, of course not. We don't have any plans. Go ahead and go. Have a good time." I felt like maybe I should take out a cigar or a pipe and light up. I sounded like somebody's father.

"He's given you permission, Sage," Bob said.

If I had had a gun right then, I would have shot myself in the foot. No, I would have shot Bob in the foot.

I glanced at him. He leaned close to Sage. So close I could smell my favorite aftershave on him. I vowed never to wear it again.

Then I looked at Sage. She smiled in such a way that I thought my heart would fall out onto the hall floor and keep right on beating. And it wasn't a clean floor, either.

"All right, then, if George and I don't have plans, I guess I'm free," Sage said.

I tried to smile, but my lips kept getting stuck on my teeth.

Sage wants to be with Bob, I thought, staring at the poster and only half-eavesdropping on the two of them. I mean, he's perfect. He's like the good-looking guy in the movies who always gets the girl. His blond hair never sticks up. His eyes are too blue to be real. He must wear colored contact lenses. I bet *he* doesn't have astigmatism.

I tried not to think about Bob, but I couldn't help it. He was right there, bigger than life, wearing my favorite after-shave and asking my best friend out on a date. I tried to

25

pretend I didn't care about what was going on right under my nose.

I'll go down to The Kalamazoo Gazette *on Friday. When she's with* him, I thought. *Maybe they could use my help getting the Sunday paper ready.* The idea made me angry. *I wanted to be with Sage.*

"All right, Bob," Sage said. "What time?"

What was wrong with me? I felt like pounding my head against the wall. No, I felt like pounding Bob's head against the wall. Why didn't I say Sage and I were doing something? I felt like gnashing my teeth. No, I felt like gnashing Bob's teeth. With my fist. But he'd kill me for sure.

"Eight-thirty. Hey, this is great, Sage. We're gonna have fun." Bob leaned toward her, smiling his white smile.

Bleaches his teeth, I thought. I pushed the tacks in hard one more time.

"Thanks, old man," Bob said to me in his ridiculous accent; then he was whistling his way down the hall. I looked at him just in time to see him wave at Sage. Then he blew her a kiss. I was incredulous.

"What a jerk," I said.

"Sounds like you're cursing, George," Sage said.

I am, I thought. *Jerk, jerk, JERK!*

The bell rang, and we hurried off toward our classes. The whole time, I fumed. How could I have been so dumb? Of course Bob would ask Sage out. Of course he would. And of course she'd say yes.

I dropped Sage off at U.S. history. Through the glass in the door, I saw Bob Taylor move his coat from the chair next to him. My heart sank when she sat down.

Sage, I thought, turning away. *Sage, you are my Angelica. I've wanted to tell you that forever, since fifth grade when you started writing romances and making me listen to them.*

You are my Angelica, and if you asked me to, I would learn to fish or become a one-eyed cameraman. I would try to be a rock singer or a rock climber or whatever that hero was a few years ago in the beginning of one of your books.

I would sell used cars, catch a thief, learn to fly a jet, become a great explorer, write classical love songs for the pan flute, do anything you wanted me to. How could I send you off with Bob Taylor? What is wrong with me?

I slammed my hand against a locker just as the bell rang. Now I was late, too.

I started feeling very depressed, because I knew in my heart of hearts that I would never be the hero Sage deserved. I went into the newspaper room, closing the door behind me with a bang.

6

How can I tell you how I feel?
You are like the movie star
who everyone wants
to be near,
and I am nothing
but an admirer
whose seat in the theater
is close to the screen
and I am not sure how I got here

7
Sage

"CHERI," I SAID. "WHAT DO YOU THINK OF IT?" I'D called Cheri after I'd finished the chapter. Cheri loves what I write, too, even better than George does, I think.

"Sage, it's wonderful," Cheri said. "What a romantic story. I absolutely love Angelica's lover. If I could find me a man like that, I'd keep him."

I laughed. "You sound thirty years old."

Cheri heaved a sigh. "What does Mr. Clinical think of this story?"

"I haven't read it to him yet." I twirled the phone cord around my finger. "I'm walking over to his house as soon as we hang up."

"I don't know what you see in him," Cheri said. "He's not a thing like any of the guys in your stories."

"To me he is," I said. Cheri and I have always had a difference of opinion about George. She doesn't see him the same way I do.

"It must be because you've known him for so long," she said. "It's blinded you or something."

I laughed a little. "I think the real reason is because I have better taste than you."

"Yeah, right," Cheri said. "What you need to do, girl,

is kiss him. If he still looks as good to you after that, then he is the man of your dreams."

"I'm not quite ready to," I said. "Kiss him, I mean. Hey, Cheri, could you hold on a second?"

Mom swept past where I sat. She wore a dress that looked like it was in style two hundred years ago. The skirt of the dress swished and crinkled. Mom's hair was piled up on her head and her bosom was squished flat. She held a pad of paper in one hand and a pen in the other.

"Research?" I asked. This is how Mom finds out how her characters feel. She always dresses up in something her characters would wear. Dad wears his dentist jacket. And normal clothes, too.

Mom didn't answer, just turned and looked at me, her eyes distant. I saw she had painted a large dark mole near her upper lip. She paused, jotted something down, and left the room.

"Okay," I said. "We were talking kisses."

"What in the world is holding you back?"

"You know me," I said.

"And you know me." Cheri doesn't even have to be introduced to a guy before she'll kiss him. I know this for a fact. I've dared her to kiss complete strangers, and she's done it. Even when they're standing with their girlfriends.

"George has to be the one to make the first move. I can't be the kisser. I have to be the kissee."

"Woman," Cheri said, "you do not know what you're missing."

After a while, we hung up. On my way over to George's, I wondered what I was missing.

Missing Kissing
Oh, George
I Am Missing
Your Kissing
Kissing Missing

I made up this poem as I walked the few houses
down to where George lives with his mom and dad.
Poetry, like Angelica prose, comes to me quite easily.

George was waiting on his front steps. The dark
wood of the door behind him made the perfect background. One of his mother's wreaths graced the door.

"Let's sit in the yard, George," I said when I got up
close to him. "I've got some great news to tell you, and
the yard is so romantic."

George raised his eyebrows at *romantic,* but he followed me to the lawn. The air was chilly, and I could
smell fireplace smoke.

"How romantic are you thinking it is, Sage?" George
asked.

"Perfectly romantic to be hearing a perfectly romantic story," I said. "The only thing better might be a fire
out on the plains."

"Huh?"

"Just listen."

"Again?"

"This is it," I said, settling myself in the leaves next
to George. "This is it. You're gonna love this one." I
started reading.

*The wind whipped grit and sand onto Angelica's once
peaches-and-cream skin. Her blond hair was a mass of curls*

that miraculously held itself in place by sheer will, even though the wind was blowing at hurricane speeds.

Angelica struggled along the buffalo trail toward California. Every step in the patent-leather lace-up boots was an agonizing one. Surely by the end of the day she would need Band-Aids for her blisters.

The twin pearl-handled Colt .45s of her dead husband hung heavy on her hips. If only she hadn't mistaken Ryan for a three-pronged antelope, they'd be making this journey together. Oh why had she been so quick to shoot? Why hadn't she noticed the bright yellow windbreaker he had been wearing, the one she wore now, the one with the single bullet hole right near her breast?

Angelica wiped away the lone tear that trickled down her dusty cheek with a white-gloved finger.

Suddenly she pulled herself up to her highest height. Angelica would not give up. No! It was not in her nature to quit when the odds were against her. She had dug a six-foot grave for her husband with her bare hands, and not broken a nail. She would make it to California come hell or high water. Nothing was going to slow her down. Nothing.

"Westward ho," she bugled softly, mimicking her dead husband's cry. "Westward ho!"

It was then that Angelica noticed the throngs of brightly painted Indians on the distant hill, their bows and arrows aimed directly at her heart.

"Oh, pooh," she grimaced.

When I looked at George I was surprised. His mouth hung open, almost resting on his chest. I could tell he loved what I had read.

"It's my best yet, isn't it?" I bowed my head. George was speechless. My lips ached from trying to hold back a smile. If I were to smile, surely I'd laugh at the beauty of my work.

I looked at George again. His mouth was still open.

"Close your mouth, George," I said. "You're beginning to look like Andrew. There's more."

His mouth bobbed open and closed a few times. Then he asked, "More to Andrew?"

"No, more to the book."

"You've written more than this?"

I couldn't hold my smile back another second. I beamed at George. "Yes! Yes! I have. Close your mouth. Remember the surprise I told you about? I started writing this yesterday in U.S. history. I stayed up all night writing. I've got almost thirteen chapters finished and more to come."

I laughed out loud. I'd never gotten this far on any of my writing before. Usually I start something and then quit because I can't think of any creative ideas. But not this time.

"George," I said, touching his arm, "George, it was like magic for me. I mean my pen practically dripped the words of Angelica's story out onto the paper all by itself." I could see myself in the reflection of George's glasses. My face moved in twin picture images, every once in a while getting caught in a tiny, bright sun reflection.

"There's an Indian in this story that—" I stopped. I had almost said "that reminds me of you." I patted a thick pile of papers at my side, all original Angelica material. "Let me read the rest of this out loud."

George moved his hands around in the fall-colored leaves like he was swimming in an ocean of orange and bright yellow.

"No," he said in a loud voice. "No! This isn't a good time. I don't have time. Remember I'm going to work?"

"Yes, I know that. But I thought that was this evening. I thought we were going to be together for the day, until my date with Bob tonight."

"You're right. But I may have a lot of things to do later. You know how hectic it is before a Sunday newspaper comes out. I probably should rest." George yawned. Sort of.

"George, if I didn't know better, I would think you don't want to hear my book."

George bowed his head, then looked at me. "You're right, Sage, I don't."

I laughed. "I'm going to put a funny character in my book who's just like you are. A tease." My George-Indian is very serious. A comic George in my book might work nicely.

"What I meant, Sage," George said, "is that there's no time for me to listen to thirteen chapters about Angelica."

"Well, okay," I said. "But I do have an idea. How about if you go lie down on the sofa and I read you into blissful slumber?"

"What?" George's voice went up high and squeaky. He sounded like a second-grader again.

"I'm thinking of ways to help you rest."

"No, Sage, not today. Angelica is too exciting to put me to sleep. So much action. Any other book would probably knock me right out." George stretched his arms way out to the sides and yawned again. Sort of. Then he stood up.

I smiled. "All right. But there's something else I

want to tell you. Something that you'll die about, when you hear it. Another surprise."

"What, Sage?" George asked. He was still standing tall, looking down at me like there was nothing more I could say that *could* surprise him. The blue of the sky peeked at me through the splotches of colorful leaves hanging on the trees. George offered me his hand and pulled me to my feet.

I couldn't stop grinning. "I'm entering this Angelica novel in the school creative-writing contest."

George's mouth dropped open again.

I kept talking. "I would never even have thought about doing it if I hadn't followed you around, posting those signs. If you hadn't had the great idea to advertise for the contest, I would never have had the great idea to submit my stuff. And then, when both you *and* Cheri told me that I should enter, I knew it was the right thing. I mean, if *you* love Angelica, so will everyone else. Isn't it wonderful? Thank you for the idea." I leaned forward a bit, wanting for a moment to rest my head on George's shoulder.

George looked like he might faint. In fact, for a little while I thought I'd have to remind him to breathe, he was so surprised. He was like a fish out of water.

Seeing him that way, with his eyes almost bulging, reminded me of Angelica's Indian lover. I pictured George without a shirt, wearing Indian garb, his hair smoothed back from his face with bear grease. I bet bear grease could hold that cowlick down. I wondered if he smelled anything like the Indian in my story.

"You can't do that, Sage," George whispered. "I won't let you. Go home. Now. But leave this Angelica story here with me."

"What do you mean? I can't leave this here. The creative juices are running."

"Flowing," George said.

"What?"

"The creative juices are flowing."

"Whatever. If I don't have my manuscript, how can I complete it?"

"Let me see if I can work out any of the bugs for you, Sage. It has a few bugs. Go on home and . . . and study. Let me get you the ACT study guide. Concentrate on the English section. And history, too. In fact, I think it's a good idea that you stop writing in U.S. history and start listening."

"Oh, George," I said, and laughed. I love to see him so surprised. "I don't need any help in English. You know that. And I've learned plenty of history from reading my mother's novels."

"Your mother writes fantasy, Sage."

"Well, it has a lot of romance in it."

"But we're talking about history, and your mother's writing is all made up."

"That'll work for me, too," I said.

George had hold of my elbow now. He ran me toward my house, four houses down from his. He moved me this way and that, squeezing my arm as he maneuvered me closer to home. With all that rushing around, though, he forgot to give me the study guide, thank goodness. I was taking lots of fast steps to keep up with him.

When we reached the picket fence that surrounds my yard, George opened the gate and pushed me through.

"Thanks for reading Angelica," I said, "though I really think I should have the manuscript to work on."

"Let the creative juices rest a bit," George said, clutching the lined paper to his chest.

"I don't know if I can. Writing by hand is such an inspiring thing." I waved goodbye to George, but he didn't wave back. He just stood there in a patch of sunlight with my book, looking at me like he'd lost his best friend. It was the weirdest thing.

I turned and went into the house. Thank goodness Mom had typed Angelica into the computer last night while watching an old Humphrey Bogart movie. She was pretending to be a scribe for the book she's working on. She can type and watch TV at the same time, and she doesn't really read what she's typing. I'm not a thing like her. Not only do I have to hunt for every key but by the time I'm through, it's like I've memorized each word I typed. Not Mom. She never remembers a thing. And anyway, to me the computer is not as romantic as colored paper and a perfumed pen.

From now on, though, I'd write Angelica the modern way instead of longhand.

8

George

SAGE HAS WANTED TO BE A FAMOUS writer ever since I can remember. Maybe because her mother is the famous Lorna Lovelocks, fantasy writer.

And Sage has never been that good at writing. Maybe because her mother is the famous Lorna Lovelocks, fantasy writer.

Let me give you a brief description of a Lorna Lovelocks novel. A single word describes it. *Steamy.* I know this because I read one. It was *Ice Princess of the Himalayas.* I'd only gotten halfway through it when Mom caught me. She told me I wasn't allowed to read such steamy novels until I had a family of my own. Then she threw the book away. I had to go to the library to finish it.

Sage's mom, Mrs. Oliver, is a good writer. Steamy, but good. Her descriptions are right on; her fantasy, believable. And I guess that's great since she has twenty-eight books out, all of them still in print.

As Sage walked up to her doorway, turning every few steps to wave at me, Mrs. Oliver came to the bay window at the front of the house and parted the curtains. I noticed she wore a dark wig. It startled me. I nodded a goodbye to her.

She raised a lit candle, like she was saying farewell and gave me a small smile.

"Mom's writing again," Sage called.

"I see that," I said.

So why hadn't Sage learned a thing or two about writing from her mother?

I thought I might hurl. I mean, that's how bad my stomach hurt. "I hope she doesn't set anything on fire with that candle."

"What?"

"Nothing."

"Are you all right?" Sage leaned out her doorway now. Mrs. Oliver disappeared from view, candle in hand. Nothing that I could see was burning.

I nodded, shook my head, then nodded again.

"Are you going to be okay?" Sage started from her front porch toward me.

"Go on in," I managed to say.

I was almost too ill to speak. I looked at the *Angelica and the Seminole Indians* manuscript in my hands. My sick stomach lurched. I walked home in slow motion and went up to my room to call Andrew.

"Hey," I said, when Andrew answered the phone. "I've got a problem." I sat down at my desk and flipped on the computer. When I'm worried, I write.

Andrew snorted. "You're not planning to complain for another hour about Sage and that Boob Taylor guy, are ya?"

"Thanks for being a friend," I said. "No, this is a real problem. A big problem."

"You got cancer."

"No."

"Then you don't have a big problem. I've told you a

million times not to exaggerate." Andrew snorted again. Sage has pointed out to me that Andrew is a snorter. You know, anytime he's disgusted with something, he sucks in air through his nose like it's his last breath. It makes Sage crazy.

"Are ya gonna listen to me, Darby, or not?" My stomach was okay now that I had argued with my friend.

"All right, all right," Andrew said. "I'm listening."

"It's about Sage."

"You just told me I wasn't going to have to listen to that story again—"

"Do you mind?" I said, interrupting him. I picked up a pencil and tapped on Angelica.

"It just better not be about that Boob Taylor guy."

"I told you I wasn't going to tell you that."

"Well then, get on with it," Andrew said with a snort.

So I got on with it. "Here's the story, Darby. Sage is gonna enter her book in the school writing contest."

Andrew laughed. A really loud, screeching laugh.

"I know why she hates your guts," I said. "Listen to the whole story, will you?"

"Okay, go on," Andrew said between what sounded like fits.

"Forget it," I said. Andrew and I have been friends a long time. We're on the track team together. And we've worked at the school paper together, too. I like him, even though he and Sage don't get along. The two don't mix, so I never make them. But Andrew is one of the smartest guys I know, so I was sure he could help me with the Angelica problem.

"I'm listening," Andrew said. "I swear I won't laugh anymore. Not where you can hear me."

"Goodbye," I said. "I'm hanging up."

"I'll be good," Andrew said. "I promise. Let me see if I can sort out the problem. Sage wants to enter her terrible writing in the school contest." He let out a huge guffaw.

I hung up the phone. I tapped my pencil and flipped through Angelica. Going over to my bed, I fell back on it and held Angelica to my chest. I thought.

"What is she doing?" I asked the ceiling. "What is Sage thinking about?"

I never realized getting her story recognized was so important to her. I mean, the Schoolcraft High School Creative Writing Contest? Competing against people like Andrew Darby? Competing against juniors and seniors? Sage wouldn't stand a chance.

"Why?" I said. "Why, why, whywhywhy?"

Last year I listened to the English teachers moan and groan about reading all the manuscripts that were submitted to the contest. That's what happens when you work on anything "scholarly." Like the newspaper. Anyway, the most sarcastic of them all is Ms. Chapin. She teaches the honors English classes and is in charge of *The Schoolcraft News*. That means I've listened to her a lot. Oh yeah, she's also the contest director.

"I won't do it," I said. There was no way I could let Sage turn in *Angelica and the Seminole Indians*. The title made my face turn warm. Seminole Indians on the plains? I shuddered. Didn't Sage remember that the Seminole Indians lived in Florida?

I took a deep breath and tried to clear my mind of the novel, trying to see how Sage might feel if she only knew how awful her story was. She'd be horrified if people didn't love her romance—didn't love Angelica. I couldn't let that happen. I cared about Sage way too much.

41

I thought of this very afternoon at school.

I thought of Bob.

"What a jerk," I said. I had worried so much about Sage's date with Bob that I'd missed quite a few mistakes in an article about whether or not vending machines should be placed in the halls of the school. I couldn't even make up a good horoscope. Ms. Chapin had watched me like I was growing tentacles or something.

"Mr. Blandford," Ms. Chapin had said.

How could anyone so mature act so hateful?

I had pointed a finger at my chest. *"Moi?"*

She ignored my small attempt at humor.

"Being the assistant editor of the school newspaper is a big job and an honor." Ms. Chapin had worked her way around some desks and was coming closer to where I sat at the computer. She held a printout of the vending-machine story in her hand. "Especially at your age. You need to always be prepared to give the facts and information that the entire student body deserves."

I nodded and watched her painted mouth move as she lectured on and on. And to think Sage and I had this person for English, too. She was enough to make sane people want to quit school.

"Get it together, George," Ms. Chapin said finally, pointing hard at me.

You look ridiculous when you put your pencil behind your ear, I thought. But all I said was, "Okay, Ms. Chapin."

She walked away and sat down at her desk, watching me the rest of that ninety-minute class period.

And I worried about Sage the rest of the period. Only, after my "chat" with Ms. Chapin, I did it while staring at the screen and not off into space like I had been. I guess I *don't* write when I'm worried. I guess I mull.

When the bell rang, I waited for Sage to come and get me from the newspaper room. We walk home together.

I was still trying to think up a few more horoscopes (I had just finished Taurus) when Sage walked in. Bob Taylor was with her. His hand rested on her shoulder. I felt all the muscles I had in my skinny body go tight.

"How about a little kiss goodbye?" he said. His voice was low, but it carried right over to my listening ears.

"No, thank you," she said, and gave him a smile that would stop a train, it was so beautiful. "Remember what I told you the last time we went out? I'm saving myself for the right guy."

I could see Bob was exasperated. "Sage, don't you think that's a little old-fashioned? I mean, what if people found out that you don't let guys kiss you?"

"I really don't care what people think about that, Bob. Or about me, for that matter. And speaking of kissing, I won't even let George kiss me, and I've known him nearly forever." She waved her hand in my direction.

I continued to pretend not to be looking or listening. But my ears tried so hard to hear everything the Jerk said to her, I thought I was going to bust an eardrum from strain.

"No one would let George kiss them, Sage. He's a geek. No offense, old man," he called to me.

Jerk, I thought, but I just looked down at the last lines I had written. *Taurus: Beware the aliens that loom in the class-rooms. All teachers have eyes in the back of their heads, so don't pick your nose and wipe anything under the desktop. Eat it instead.*

"I don't appreciate your talking like that about my friend, Bob." Sage was pretty angry. Very pretty angry. I liked it. I watched out of the corner of my eye, ears stretching in her direction.

"Hey, I'm not trying to be unkind," Bob said.

Yeah, right, I thought.

"But you know the old saying: 'Newspaper writers are geeks.'" Bob laughed. "I made that up. Hey, I gotta go to football practice, Sage. I'll pick you up tonight about eight-fifteen or so." He leaned toward her, but Sage turned and walked to where I sat.

"Ignore him, George," she said to me, her voice loud. "He's speaking with his hormones."

I nodded. I understood the way Bob felt.

All day I had worried about Sage going on another date with Bob. I thought the worst thing that could happen, had.

Now, lying in my bedroom, I knew there *was* something worse than Sage going out with Bob Taylor. It was Sage turning in her Angelica book to the school contest.

At last I couldn't stand it anymore.

"Mom, Dad," I called. "I'm going into work for a while to see if they need me."

Mom watched *Jeopardy!* with Dad. That's one thing that binds my parents together: television. They love competing on the game shows with each other, and they love watching documentaries, and they love laughing at old shows. Thank goodness they have TV in common or maybe my mother would wander around the house in weird costumes and wearing wigs like Sage's mother does.

"All right," they called at the same time.

I went outside and got on my bike. It was a mile and a half to the newspaper building. I'm a copy clerk at *The Kalamazoo Gazette.* Copy clerk sounds like a pretty important job, but really it's a fancy name for gofer. I run errands between desks and floors and generally do the things the writers and editors don't have time to do. I like my job. It's interesting, and all my work here at this paper has gotten me the position of assistant editor on the high-school newspaper.

"What do I do?" I said, my voice matching the rhythm of my bike's tires. "What do I do?"

I'd see the teachers every day.

I'd hear them talk about the entries.

I'd hear comments about Angelica and the ridiculous Seminole Indians.

"Help me, help me," I said to my bike and the trees and the cool evening air. "Think, think, think." I thought, thought, thought.

What could *I* do?

"I'm only a peon sophomore," I said, my voice a mumble. "What am I supposed to do? Walk into the teachers' lounge, swimming through the cigarette smoke, and demand that Sage's novel be removed from the contest?" Hmmm, now that was an idea.

Ms. Chapin's likeness floated in my head. I envisioned her laughing at my request. In my imagination, her face became so large I could ride my bike down the tunnel of her throat. I shook my head. I wouldn't be demanding anything from *her* too soon.

There had to be another way of keeping Sage from putting her novel into the contest. My mind reeled.

Maybe now that I had part of *Angelica and the Seminole Indians,* I could figure out what to do.

9

I could protect you if
waving my words was like wielding a sword
I would be your knight
in print
And save the princess
from those who offend
with a slicing comma,
and an ending period.
Then place her safely
in a poem
where all the words rhyme
and the rhythm is perfect.

10
Sage

Angelica performed CPR on her Indian lover. His lips were blue. Both of his eyes were closed. At least Angelica thought they were. One eye was covered by a bearskin eye patch. The other lay limply in its socket.

"Do not die, damn you!" Angelica howled at the moon. Then one, two, three, four, five. Breath. Breath. One, two, three, four, five. Breath. Breath.

Angelica's perfectly curled hair trembled with fear. Her white-gloved hands looked even whiter on her lover's bare chest.

"Get up, 247 Bears. Get up!" Angelica yodeled like an American Indian banshee.

Suddenly the piece of deer meat spewed forth from his mouth. The dark-haired man breathed deeply, then stood on his own two feet.

Angelica, *he signed to her.* You have saved me. Will you be my squaw?

Angelica, kneeling at his feet, read the signs, impatiently at first, then triumphantly.

Yes, *she signed back fluently. Her skill with the language was like her skill with CPR.*

247 Bears' scarred face quivered. His lone brown eye

glittered with happiness. He nodded his head once, then turned to prepare the tepee.

I could not contain my own happiness. Why, what I was feeling was only a hair's breadth less than what 247 Bears felt. I heaved a great sigh.

My first real novel was going so well that excitement bubbled in my chest. Every once in a while a bubble would pop and my stomach would flip-flop.

George looked miserable. He sat on the sofa in my living room, his head resting on the rose-patterned cushions. He clenched and unclenched his hands.

"Do you have a cold?" I asked him. I felt overcome with compassion. I would take care of George forever, nursing him through all his illnesses.

"Let me make you something to eat." I got up from where I sat next to him. Angelica would never allow 247 Bears to go hungry. Had he not almost choked to death on the venison Angelica's delicate, gloved hands had prepared? I, like Angelica, would care for the man in my life.

An idea popped into my mind. Why, I could do what Mom does. Dress the part. I could dress in a satin gown like Angelica's and feed George. That way I would know exactly what it felt like to be Angelica, what it felt like to cook for an Indian.

"We don't have any deer meat or buffalo," I said. "How does Campbell's sound?" Would George wear an eye patch if I asked him to? Or better yet, a loincloth?

George rolled his head back and forth. Probably not.

I heard a snicker, but I didn't know where it had come from. Morgan was hiding again, listening in on my conversation with George.

48

"No, thank you, Sage," George said, not opening his eyes. "I don't have a cold."

"You look kind of sick." I put my hand on George's forehead and glanced around the room. Where was that little sneak? Sometimes he made me so mad. I've talked to Mother about Morgan invading my privacy, but she thinks it's cute. That's what happens when you have one sibling almost eight years younger than you. Your parents think everything they do is adorable.

I looked back at George. He felt fine, though his forehead started to get sweaty under my touch. I decided to ignore Morgan, wherever he was.

"I am sick," George said. "But it's nothing food can cure."

"Tell me where you're sick, George. I'm sure I could help you feel better." I smiled right in his face.

When we grow old together, I'll take care of George. He won't even have to tell me what's wrong. I'll know. I'll tuck him into our bed and pull the teal and peach comforter around his neck. I'll move my computer into our room and read each and every chapter of Angelica to him, as soon as it's written, to help him recuperate.

"Sage, listen." George leaned forward with a sigh and took hold of my hands. A bubble in my chest popped. I smiled bigger. George looked hard at me. I leaned forward a bit. Maybe a small kiss for the one I love wouldn't hurt. It would definitely help my research. It was while I leaned toward him that I noticed the tiny specks of gold in George's eyes.

"Whoa," I said.

"What?"

Morgan mimicked me with a muffled "Whoa."

Both George and I looked around the room.

"An Angelica idea just struck me," I said. And what an idea. I jumped off the sofa and ran for the kitchen. On the blackboard I scribbled: *Angelica and 247 Bears Pan for Gold Together! They Find Mine!!!*

"Oh my gosh," I said, coming back into the living room. "These ideas are pouring from me like water from a pump." I stopped near the sofa. "Hey, that's a good line." I ran back into the kitchen and jotted that down, too.

Coming back into the living room, I plopped on the sofa next to George. "Can you believe this?" I asked. "Can you actually believe it? Now I know how all the famous writers felt. Hemingway, Faulkner, Steinbeck, and O'Connor. When you have the mood, the words flow."

George fell back and rocked his head on the sofa cushion again. He opened his mouth once or twice.

"What, George?"

"What, George," came a muffled voice.

"Sage, I don't know how to tell you this," George said.

"Sage, I don't know how to tell you this."

I glanced around, trying to find Morgan.

"What?" I asked.

"What?"

"It's about Angelica."

"It's about Angelica."

A compliment! I felt my face would crack wide open with the smile that stretched across it.

"Angelica needs to perform the Heimlich maneuver on the Indian guy, not CPR. He's choking, you know. Not that first-aid techniques like that were even invented way back then."

Morgan made gagging noises.

George stood up.

"Morgan," he said. "Where are you hiding?" George was not using his happy voice.

"Ignore him, George," I said. I bit my bottom lip. "You're right. Do you think anyone will notice that one little mistake when the book is read as a whole?"

"There are other mistakes, so maybe it won't stick out. But Sage, you should try and make this your best writing if you're still planning on submitting it to the contest." George looked at me with his brown-and-gold eyes. "*Are* you still planning on submitting this story?"

"Of course. Why not? And when I told Mom I was going to, *she* got all excited. Two writers in the same family. We went and bought some paper together. A ream, you know."

"Has your mom read Angelica yet?" George asked.

"Well, she's looked at it. But she's saving the reading till I win. Then she'll come over to school and listen to it there. Every morning."

George's eyes rolled back into his head.

"Let's talk about this little problem," I said. "Except for that one teeny thing, what do you think?" I didn't wait for an answer. "*I* think this is my absolute best. I'm *very* proud of this. In fact, George, I'm thinking of submitting it to a real publisher after the school contest."

George closed his eyes and swallowed.

"What?" he asked in a soft voice.

"Maybe my mom's. But let's not think too, too far ahead."

I could tell by looking at him that George is my biggest fan. I'm his, too.

"Sage has got another boyfriend," came a whiny

voice. There! Morgan's toes stuck out from behind the drapes near the window.

I walked over to where he was hiding and jerked back the flowered material.

"Hello," Morgan said.

"Go on up to your room. You know what Mother said about you interrupting my life."

"Yes," said Morgan. "She said it was natural for a boy my age to spy on his older sister because I look up to you and want to be like you."

"She also said you're to leave me alone. I can listen in on your conversations, too. Now go."

Morgan took his time crossing the thick blue carpet.

"But aren't you going to kiss each other?" he asked, wiggling his bottom as he walked. "Like they do on TV?"

George looked like he felt a little better. "Should we, Morgan?"

"Not you and me," Morgan said, and he made a cross of two fingers and pointed it at George.

George laughed. "No. Should Sage and I kiss?"

"Can I watch if you do?" Morgan asked.

"Absolutely not," I said. "Get out."

"No, wait, Morgan. I have a question for you," George said.

"Don't give him a reason to stay." I wanted to talk about Angelica. I went and sat in a wingback chair.

"No really, it's okay." George patted the sofa next to himself. "Let's visit, old pal."

Morgan hurried over to George.

"Does Sage kiss the other guys she brings in here?" George asked, grinning big at me. He moved his eyebrows up and down a few times.

"You might not like the answer," I said. "You just might not."

"Uh-uh," said Morgan, shaking his head. "But they all try to kiss her. Isn't that gross?"

George nodded. He looked a little tight-lipped. I knew he wouldn't like the answer.

"It sure is gross. Now what about the Boob guy?"

Morgan screeched with laughter. "The Boob guy," he said. "The Boob guy."

"Well?" George asked.

"There aren't any guys with boobs that come here." Morgan laughed so hard, I thought he might fall off the sofa.

"No," George said. "I mean Bob Taylor."

"Oh, him. Yeah, he really tries. At least he did the other night."

I stood up, my hands on my hips. "I don't like it when you spy on me, Morgan," I said. "I feel furious."

"What was that?" George asked. "What did he try?"

"Goodbye, Morgan," I said. "And that's none of your business, George."

Morgan looked sideways at me. "He pushed her down on the sofa and everything."

George jumped to his feet, and I sat back down.

"You're the only one who never tries anything with Sage," Morgan said.

"What do you mean by 'anything'?" George asked. His voice sounded a little like steam coming from a teakettle.

Morgan shrugged. "That's what Sage always says. I keep watching to see if anything ever happens, but it doesn't."

"Have you learned enough yet?" I asked George. "I would like him to leave."

"I like you the best, George," Morgan said.

"Yeah?" George asked.

"Yeah. Funny stuff happens when you're around. Sage reads that dumb book about kissing to you, and you roll your eyes and make weirdo faces when she's not looking."

"Time for you to run on to your room," George said. He jerked Morgan up and gave him a shove toward the door.

"What funny faces?" I asked. "You make funny faces while I'm reading?"

"Not always," said Morgan. "Sometimes he shakes his head a lot."

"From happiness," George said to me. "Goodbye, Morgan. Want to go to the movies with us again sometime soon?"

"Yeah!" said Morgan. "Will you take me to a scary show? Sage is afraid to go to those."

"We'll see." George smiled a big fake smile. "If you go right now."

A horn beeped outside, and Morgan leaped off the sofa and ran out of the room, screeching, "Daddy's home! Daddy's home!"

"Such a cute kid," George said. He did have a weirdo look on his face.

"George, do you like *Angelica and the Seminole Indians*? Be honest."

George didn't answer. Instead he asked, "Sage, what all does Boob try with you? The jerk."

I moved close to George and looked up at him. I

touched his arm and imagined him in Indian garb. *Would he be willing to wrestle a bear for me?* I wondered.

I wanted to rest my head on George's chest. But I didn't. Instead I said, "George, I am waiting for my own Indian lover."

He smiled at me, a nice slow smile. "How," he said.

I laughed. "Oh, George, Indians don't say things like that." I stepped back a bit and picked up my manuscript where I'd left it on the floor. "Now tell me: Do you like *Angelica and the Seminole Indians?*"

George let out a great sigh, then closed his eyes. *"Kemosabe."*

"Tell me, George."

"Sage," George said, opening his eyes, then moving to sit on the sofa. "Before I answer that question, let me ask *you* one. Would you stop writing just because I said I didn't like it?"

"No, of course not," I said. "I never have before."

"I see." George took a deep breath. "I like this book about as much as I have liked any of your other Angelica stories."

I beamed at him. "That's what I thought."

11

George

WHEN I LEFT SAGE'S PLACE, I THOUGHT hard about what to do with Angelica. I was burdened with more Angelica than I could stand.

Somehow this character had become a living being. She'd been alive since the fifth grade, doing incredible, unbelievable, ridiculous things.

I looked down at the sheaf of papers in my hand and flipped through a few pages.

. . . the tiny diamonds were glued to her long fingernail tips. . . .

. . . Angelica grabbed ahold of the buffalo's horn with a gloved hand and in a single bound pulled herself aboard. . . .

. . . one-eyed Indian slithered, wrapping himself snake-like up the tree, hiding in the . . .

I closed my eyes, shaking my head.

"Angelica. I've got to get rid of you. But how?"

I looked at the manuscript. No answer.

"Come on, Angelica. You'd know what to do."
I turned to near the end of the partial book.

. . . Angelica, naked except for her Lady Godiva–type hair, galloped across the plains, her firm . . .

"What?" I burst out. Maybe this book wasn't quite what I'd thought. I flipped to the next page.

. . . her firm grip on the saddle horn never ceasing despite the spray of arrows and bullets that echoed in the dark night around her . . .

Oh. "Come on, Blandford, think what to do. What can you do?"
I was home now.
I paced up and down the driveway. I didn't want to go in where Mom and Dad were enjoying fine literature together. Oh, all right. They were watching TV, but I still didn't want to go in.
I sat down on the bumper of Dad's Jeep. "I could rewrite the whole thing." No, that wouldn't work. There wasn't enough time, and that was cheating.
"Hide Angelica in my room and set fire to the house." Hmmm. Probably not a good idea. Not after all the decorating Mom had done, getting things just the way she liked them. If I burned down our house to get rid of Angelica, my parents would be unhappy with me.
"Earthquake?" I shook my head. That was plain dumb. If I could control the elements, maybe. But the chances of an earthquake happening in our area are slim. Of course, there could be a nuclear war. Hey, now that's an idea.

"I can only hope," I said, and walked inside the house. But knowing how much Sage loved Angelica, I'd be expected to save my half of the novel despite radioactive fallout.

There are no nearby volcanoes, so I couldn't sacrifice the manuscript to the novel gods.

Thieves do not usually steal handwritten manuscripts.

I went into the living room. Mom and Dad snuggled on the sofa, watching a documentary. The light from the TV shone a bit on Dad's bald head.

"Hello, George," Mom said. "Want to come in and watch this with us?"

"No, thanks. I'm going up to bed."

"Good night," my parents said.

I walked upstairs and went in the bathroom to shower. Then I climbed into bed. I thought of Sage standing close, so close I could see the tiny curls near her forehead. I could even smell her breath. Spearmint. Her breath was spearmint.

I lay in bed thinking of Sage. If she weren't waiting for the right guy, I would have kissed her. There in her living room, with Morgan watching. Why didn't I know some more Native American words? I couldn't fall asleep. I got up and went to call Andrew.

"It's me, Darby," I said, when he got on the phone.

"I'm busy," he said.

"Doing what?"

"Thinking."

"Having any severe headache pain?"

"Ha, ha," Andrew said, and then he snorted. "Hey, Blandford, tell me something."

"All right. It's best to chew cheeseburgers instead of swallowing bites whole like you do." I settled into my desk chair and turned on a game of FreeCell on my computer. I could hear the low hum of the TV coming from downstairs.

"You're a genius, Blandford," Andrew said. "I'm wondering a couple of things."

"The end of the world is near." It seemed that way to me.

Darby ignored that comment. "Why aren't you entering this contest? You're one of the best writers I know."

"Don't get out much, huh?"

"I've read your stuff. I've been in English with you. I see what you contribute to the paper."

"Your point?"

"You need to enter."

"Well, I'm not going to."

"Not even if we put a little money on it?" Darby asked.

"You've got the contest rigged, don't you?"

"Blandford, your intelligence amazes me. I think you and I could sweep the contest if we both entered. The idea of a sweep is worth losing a little money."

I sighed. Sage popped into my mind, and I felt a bit of happiness; then Angelica-like fear ran through me. "Don't wanna."

"Do it anyway. What have you got to lose? If you enter and don't win, no big deal. But if you win, or place even, I'll give you twenty bucks. That's a few hours of work at the *Gazette*."

I thought for a moment. Twenty bucks was enough for Sage and me to go out to dinner. "All right," I said. "I'll do it."

"Money's gonna be your downfall if you're always *that* easy to convince."

"Shut up," I said.

Andrew laughed and then snorted. That combination

would have driven Sage mad. "There's something else I want to know. It's about Sage."

"Darby, you got a crush on her, too?" I asked. I'm surprised that the entire male student body and staff at school aren't in love with her. I mean, *I* am.

"She's not that great, Blandford. I've been telling you that for ages."

"You don't know nuthin'," I said, relieved. Not that Sage would even be interested in Andrew.

"Doesn't Sage know that one girl—that Cheri Peterson girl?"

I felt my eyebrows rise on their own. "No way," I said. "No way."

"Does she or doesn't she?"

"No way, Darby. You're a nutcase if you're interested in her at all. Haven't you ever seen her shoes?"

"What?" Andrew asked.

"Man, you've gone schizo on me."

"Don't tell me how to live my social life. You are, after all, smitten by Sage Oliver."

I paused a moment. I do *not* understand Andrew Darby. He must be blind.

"Anyway, Blandford, to each his own."

"But—" I said.

Andrew slammed the phone down and the line went quiet.

I got up and made my way back to bed.

I couldn't believe Darby even had a thought in his intellectual head about Cheri Peterson. She had about as many brains as a gnat. What did he see in her? A shiver went down my spine.

I was settling down to sleep when I noticed *Angelica*

resting on my bedside table. Would Angelica ever die? Was she immortal, continuing across the country, never aging, always living, living, living? It kind of reminded me of the never-changing Nancy Drew and Hardy Boys.

That night I dreamed that Angelica loomed around every corner. Sometimes she had blond hair, sometimes red, sometimes black. At one corner, she was bald and the light from a TV documentary reflected off her head. Every time she opened her mouth words spilled out, written in pink ink, onto the ground. I was knee-deep in them. I woke up sweating.

It was dark out. I got up and looked from my window toward Sage's house. Outside, the bare trees moved in a slight wind that grew stronger. There was very little moon, but still I could see leaves blowing into the street and then away.

"If only those leaves were Angelica," I said. "Blowing to the ends of the earth. Then I could sleep."

But Sage would feel awful if I let Angelica blow away. A gnawing came up in my stomach that seemed to grab me every time I thought of Angelica. I got back into bed, pulling the covers up to my chin. *Oh, Sage,* I thought. *Why do I have to love you so much? Why did I have to break the best-friend rule? If I didn't care, then this Angelica thing wouldn't be driving me crazy.*

"All right," I said aloud, sitting up in bed, the covers falling around my waist. "I can only do what I can do. Nothing more." I flopped back onto my pillow. And that's when it hit me like a ton of bricks. Why, it was so simple, this getting rid of Angelica. Why hadn't I thought of it before?

After I'd made my decision, I slept like a baby.

. . .

Sunday I immersed myself in homework, skipping church and working in my room until Mom asked me to join her and Dad at the table for dinner.

Only then was I able to relax, listening to Dad talk about his job at the community college, where he teaches communications and other classes. Dad's dark hair is thinning, but he doesn't grow it long on one side and comb it over his head like some men do. He keeps it short, and sometimes he jokes about polishing his head like you would an apple.

Mom is a little chubby. Her dark hair grows to her shoulders and is getting gray at the temples. Dad says she looks distinguished and tells her he doesn't want her to color it. Mom works as a decorator part-time. One of her favorite things to do is make custom wreaths. She loves working with people. She likes pleasing them with her artistic abilities.

Tonight Dad had Mom and me laughing about a girl in his Media and Arts class who always writes papers with amazing dedications.

"The dedications," Dad said, "are so good, I read her papers first 'cause I know I'll be entertained for a whole five minutes before I start into the drudgery of reading other people's work."

Angelica, I thought. *Dad would think Angelica is drudgery.*

"Give us an example," Mom said, picking up a chicken leg and taking a bite out of it.

Dad thought for a moment. "Okay, she started one paper something like this: 'I dedicate this paper to Coca-Cola, truly the real thing, that helped keep me awake so I could get through the boring article I had to read, and then through the paper I had to write. If it were not for this most amazing drink, I would still be slumped in slumber over my computer, typing out *zzzz*'s with my nose.' " Dad laughed at the memory, and so did Mom and I.

It kind of reminded me of Sage's writing. Remembering what I was going to do with Angelica made my stomach grumble with fear and, funny enough, made me feel only a little guilty and a lot relieved.

My plan: to out-and-out lie.

12

I have waited for you to know
since I was very young.
I have waited for you to
see my heart as it really is.
I have waited for you
breathless, each day.
I have waited
for you to be beside me.
I have
longed to stay near you.
I
alone
have waited for you to know.

13

Sage

I CLEARED MY THROAT TWICE BEFORE GEORGE looked at me. Then I straightened the stack of papers on the table. I could almost imagine my hands hidden in delicate white gloves. I could almost smell the earthiness of damp soil. I could lift a chunk of gold of any size.

"I've done something different this time." George, Cheri, and Andrew sat around me at the table. My stack of Angelica was piled in front of me. "I've added a few exclamation points. Imagine them as you listen."

Cheri nodded, then winked at Andrew, who stared at her. George smiled.

"How do we imagine an exclamation point?" Andrew asked, but I ignored him.

Placing my fingertips on my throat in a very Angelica-like way, I began to read.

Before her very blue eyes, Angelica spied a lump of gold the size of her left foot!

"263 Bears!" she called! "Hurry! I think we have struck it rich!" Angelica could barely lift the gold out of the hole! Digging with her bare hands had proved successful! It was

65

all the practice she had gotten while burying her first husband! Angelica wiped a lone tear from her eye, remembering! Then she called for 263 Bears again!

Suddenly! Angelica raised her head! Her nostrils flared! A familiar odor floated through the air, tickling Angelica under her nose! It smelled like . . . like Thieving White Men!

Angelica lugged the large piece of gold up out of the hole! Her eyes were dazzled by the shining gold stuff that lay under her find! Quickly she filled the cavernous hole with loose dirt, then laid oak leaves over it, to hide it from the Thieving White Men! She placed the gold into her apron pocket (she always wore her apron when she worked) and began walking light-footed to where she had last seen 263 Bears!

Angelica gasped!! There he was, her beloved, tied to a stake! Two bearded Thieving White Men held 263 Bears captive!

How brave a brave was he! Angelica thought! If she had even a moment to spare, Angelica would have whipped out her pen and begun the poem that she saw in 263 Bears!

Oh Bear Man of mine!
With fourteen-karat-gold spine!

Wait! Angelica thought! The poem was good, but she didn't have a moment to spare! Reaching into her pocket, Angelica withdrew the piece of gold! Settling it into her hand, she threw it shot put–like, setting a new world's record!

Her aim was accurate! The gold hit the first Thieving White Man in the head, then ricocheted and smacked the

*other in the face! Both fell to the ground as if they were
dead!*

I closed my eyes and took in a deep breath. I was in
gold country with Angelica and 263 Bears. I didn't want
to come back to school at all.

"Couldn't you almost hear music playing as this
scene took place?" I asked the three of them, my eyes
still closed. "I'm wondering if I'll be allowed to help
write the screenplay. You know, for the miniseries."

A snort sounded, and I jerked my eyes open. Of
course, Andrew. He was the only Thieving White Man
at the table.

"Sage," Cheri said, and let out a big breath. "Oh,
Sage, that was perfect. What's going to happen next? I
can't wait to hear more."

"Well, I'm thinking that Angelica and 263 Bears will
escape with all their gold. They may start their own
Native American business." I glanced at George.

He sat across the table from me, smiling.

But not the Thieving White Man. "What?" Andrew
screeched, his voice so loud people at the next two tables
looked over at us. "They're going to move *all* the gold?"

Cheri reached across the table. "Andrew," she said,
resting her hand on his. "This is a *love* story."

The Thieving White Man looked from Cheri's hand
to her face, then back to her hand again. He didn't say
anything, but his lips quivered.

"In a love story," Cheri said, "the hero is so strong he
could teach Hercules a thing or two."

"Oh," the Thieving White Man said, still looking at
Cheri's hand. "I see what you mean."

Cheri has that kind of effect on every guy she dates. George can't understand it, but I can. It's sex appeal. It's the very thing that makes Angelica so adorable.

"Right," I said to Cheri. "You're a natural editor."

I turned to George. He was still smiling.

Cheri stood. "I've got to get outta here. I have to take a make-up test in math. Are you coming, Andrew, or staying?"

Andrew jumped over his chair and practically fell on his face trying to get to Cheri, who looked back at me and waved goodbye.

"What do *you* think of it, George?"

He didn't say anything. Right behind him, on a bulletin board, was one of the large signs we had posted together a few weeks earlier. I had chosen this place to sit so I could be inspired by it.

Enter Schoolcraft High's
Fourth Annual Writing Contest
Open to ALL STUDENTS
Deadline for submissions: November 15

"I have two weeks to finish my book," I told George. He still looked at me, still smiled, his head propped on his hand. His stare was so intense that I felt my face start to flush.

"What?" I demanded. "What? Stop it. Why are you looking at me like that?" I laughed a little.

George kept smiling. It was a soft smile. A one-eyed 263 Bears smile.

"Are you almost finished with *Angelica and the Seminole Indians*?" he asked.

"Well, I'm not sure," I said, ignoring his look and

straightening the thick pile of pages. I had written fourteen more chapters. My novel was going to be a saga. A monumental amount of work completed by a fifteen-year-old. I would be on all the talk shows. I wondered if George would travel with me when I toured the country. I could see myself in New York, sitting in front of blinding studio lights while all my fans waved their copies of *Angelica* at me.

"When are you giving back the rest of my book so I can put this all together?" I asked. "I'd like to have it bound before I hand it in. I do think the handwritten version is so romantic." My voice sounded dreamy, even to my own ears. I like dreamy.

"Soon," George said, looking away like something had surprised him. He stood up. "Let's get to English. We're going to be late."

George didn't wait for me. I followed, trotting along, until we got to class. We slid into our chairs and listened while Ms. Chapin began another boring lecture on Mark Twain. I don't know why she couldn't just let us read some of the things he'd written. Some of the things we *wanted* to read. No, she had to lecture the entire forty-five minutes. What a grouch. She never even smiled when she talked. Not only that, but we had assigned seats in this class. Thank goodness Cheri was in here with George and me, or I would have been bored out of my skull. Not that we all get to sit together. Chapin had already separated the three of us, sending George way across the room. She said we talked too much.

Cheri and I were still close enough that we could communicate via note and finger spelling, two things we had been doing forever. I decided to drop her a line.

Hey!
What do you think Chapin will think of my book? Wouldn't it be funny if in five years, she was preaching about Angelica? Think she'd still frown?
Me

I squished the note small and tossed it onto Cheri's desk. A few minutes later she answered.

Dear Me,
I would give my right arm to hear her critique your book. She'll croak when she finds out she has a publishable authoress in her class. And it will be soooo cool to listen to you read over the intercom. Especially those steamy parts. Don't forget to breathe heavy there.
C.

I had just bent down to write my answer when Ms. Chapin came up and took the note.

"Aaah, a little correspondence," she said, "between two of our pupils. Shall we share this with the class, Ms. Oliver?"

"Why not, Ms. Chapin?" I said, shrugging. "It's a G-rated note." A few kids in the class giggled. It was plain to see that everybody was bored to tears. Too bad I hadn't been working on my Angelica story at the moment. The class needed a bit of livening up.

Ms. Chapin read the note, then smiled a fake smile at Cheri and me. Her jaw worked. It was clear she was unhappy. No matter how bored her students are, Ms. Chapin hates it when anyone does anything except stare right at her during her lectures.

"Ms. Oliver," she said, "*you* are entering the contest this year? How exciting. I cannot wait to read your . . . what are you doing?"

"A novel," Cheri said. "A romance novel."

A thrill ran through my stomach. It was one thing to think of the novel myself, but to hear someone else talk about it like that? And out loud in front of thirty-something people? My face turned pink. I bowed my head. Could everyone in the room hear my heart pounding?

"So, Ms. Peterson," Ms. Chapin said. "You are now Ms. Oliver's spokesperson?"

I decided right then and there to add Chapin to my novel as a greasy, dirty moneymonger. She'd be missing teeth.

"As necessary," Cheri said. "And very possibly her editor. Maybe her agent, even."

Ms. Chapin turned away. "May I tell you how delighted I am that I get to read and judge your creative efforts, Ms. Oliver? And you, Ms. Peterson? Are *you* submitting a world-shaking masterpiece also?"

"Are you kidding? No way," Cheri said. "But rumor has it Mr. Blandford might be."

Ms. Chapin looked toward George. "Is this so?"

George cleared his throat, then said, "I've been thinking about it."

I was surprised.

"Excellent." Ms. Chapin moved back to her desk and sat down. "Regardless of the fact that I am one of the readers for this year's contest, I do not want you practicing any kind of writing in class except when I tell you to do so. Is that clear, Ms. Oliver?"

I nodded.

"Ms. Peterson?"

Cheri smiled and raised her eyebrows as if to say, "You can count on me."

"Just to be sure, do you understand my rules, Mr. Blandford?"

"Yes, I do," George said.

"Is there anyone here who feels left out?"

There were a few giggles and the sound of feet shuffling, but that was it.

"Then let's continue this lecture." And Ms. Chapin was off again, talking about stuff no one could be interested in, probably including herself.

All right, George! I started another note as soon as Ms. Chapin turned to write on the board. *Maybe we'll tie for first place.*

I passed this note to Cheri, who sent it over to Wendy Rogers, who passed it over to John Caka, who passed it on back to Nile Cole, who gave it right to George.

Just by looking at his face I could see he was more than excited about the upcoming competition between the two of us.

14
George

I STACKED *ANGELICA AND THE SEMINOLE Indians* into a neat pile, then placed the partial manuscript in a manila envelope. I have to admit I felt a bit nervous.

When we moved to Maple Lane, Mom and Dad decided to buy our house because it's in a nice neighborhood, and because there was growth potential. I've heard them talk. I know this is true. Over the years our family has stayed the same size, the three of us, and I've listened to my parents make plans about what they'll do to the house when their ship comes in. You know, like finishing the basement and adding a sunroom. More things for Mom to decorate. Dad has even thought of making an office for himself in the basement—and Mom a work area so she can spread out all her things and do artsy-craftsy stuff at home.

I guess our ship missed the dock because, except for a few coats of paint and changing the carpet once and doing over window coverings, our house has also remained the same. Lucky for me. I had decided to hide Angelica, bound and hopefully gagged, in a manila envelope in our basement.

No one would ever be able to find her. All we have there is a water heater, the furnace, the washer and dryer, and a bunch of boxes full of junk. So much junk that you almost can't walk through. I'm sure it's a fire hazard, and therefore, it made the perfect hiding place.

When I came up the stairs empty-handed, I remembered Sage reading to me a few days earlier in the library with Cheri and Andrew. I could see Sage's face, so alive with that darned Angelica. Why couldn't she see that her writing wasn't good? Still, I smiled at the memories. Sage blushing with pride. And Andrew. Watching him trail Cheri like a puppy. That was worth a smile, or maybe even a guffaw.

By the time I made it upstairs to my bedroom, where my homework waited for me, I was overcome with guilt. How could I deceive my best friend in the whole world? Not just my best friend, but, well, the girl I was totally and completely in love with.

Thinking that I loved Sage made my face turn red with pleasure. Almost as soon as I blushed, I was hit with another wave of guilt.

Exercise, I thought. *I need some exercise.* I ran out of the house, grabbing my coat as I went and hollering to my parents (who were watching a rerun of *Wheel of Fortune*) that I was going to see Andrew. I got on my bike and began the long stretch over to his house.

It was sure cold. I guess that's early winter in Michigan for you. The wind kept pulling tears from my eyes. In my hurry I hadn't gotten any gloves, and my fingers froze into a handlebar-gripping shape. I wondered briefly what jobs I could get with my hands deformed like that and then wondered if Sage would still like me. Probably. Every lover Angelica had, wore an eye patch. Things could be worse. I imagined myself one-eyed, wearing a hairy Angelica bear-

skin eye patch, and at long last, pulled into the Darbys'
driveway.

Oh, blessed retreat. Smoke flowed from the chimney.
Things should be nice and warm when I got inside. I
knocked. There was no answer. *If* I got inside, I mean.

I pounded on the door. At last Andrew opened up for
me.

"What?" he said, blocking my way into his house.

"What do you mean, 'what'?" I asked, and tried to push
my way inside.

"I mean what are you doing here?"

"Freezing my butt off. Let me in."

"No way," Andrew said. "I'm busy."

I pulled my head down a bit into my jacket and eyed
Andrew.

"Darby," I said. "You've got a girl in there."

"No, I don't," Andrew said.

"Then why do you look so guilty? It's not because your
best friend is freezing on your front porch."

"Nope, it's not," Andrew said.

"Then why?"

"I'm busy."

"Look, let me in. I'll thaw, and then I'll leave," I said, and
pushed past him.

The inside of his house was so warm, for a minute my
hands and face felt like I'd splashed hot water on them. I
went into the living room.

There was no one there.

"Okay, fess up," I said. "Where is she?"

"Where is who?"

"Cheri Peterson."

"She's not here," Andrew said. "But . . ."

"But what?"

"No 'but whats.' "

"She's coming, isn't she?" I smacked my hands together, then went and warmed myself by the fire. "She's coming to sit in front of this fire with you."

Andrew didn't say anything.

"Darby, I'm overcome," I said as my fingers began to thaw.

"Me too," he said. He sounded a little funny. And I don't mean the ha-ha kind of funny, either.

"What are *you* overcome with?" I plopped down on the floor and let my back soak in the heat. It was a long way home. I'd be pedaling into the wind. "Guilt, too?"

"Not yet," Andrew said. "But I hope to be."

I raised my eyebrows. "She's not that kind of a girl."

"She's a kisser. That's good enough for me."

"I don't even want to know," I said. And I meant it. There were more important things running through my mind, and none of them had to do with Cheri's or Andrew's lips. "I was wondering if maybe you could help me get rid of the novel."

"Novel? What are you talking about?"

"Sage," I said.

"Sage?"

"Sage. And, you know, Angelica. Her book that she read to you and Cheri and me."

"Are you nuts, Blandford? Sage and Angelica are the last things on my mind."

"I believe that," I said. I felt let down. Here I needed my best guy friend's support and Andrew was thinking of a girl. And not just any girl, either.

Right then the doorbell rang.

"It's her," Andrew said, leaping so high I thought he might hit the ceiling.

"Can I get this one?" Andrew's mom called from the kitchen.

"All right," Andrew hollered.

"Hey," I said. "You told her not to let me in."

"I've got priorities," he said. "Now get out."

"What? I'm enjoying the fire and—"

Andrew grabbed hold of my arm so hard, I thought maybe he had jerked it out of its socket.

"Go out through the kitchen. I don't want her to see you here."

"Are you kidding?" I said. "I've known Cheri Peterson a lot longer than you have."

"But you're not her favorite person," Andrew said, and with a shove he pushed me into the kitchen. "I don't want to spoil the mood by her seeing you."

"Some friend," I said, and let myself out.

The whole cold way home I thought about Sage and Angelica, separated because they knew me, and Cheri and Andrew, together because they knew me. I felt a little depressed by the time I got to my street. I tried riding back and forth in front of Sage's house. I thought it might make me feel better. But it didn't. In fact, the only thing it did for me was make me so cold, I didn't think I'd ever be able to talk again. My face was frozen.

I rode home, parked my bike, and went inside. The phone rang.

It's Sage, I thought. Now I was frozen by fear and guilt. *She knows I've hidden her manuscript.* I couldn't make myself answer. I stood there in the hall, my heart pounding, my hand vibrating on the phone each time it rang.

"George," my mother called, "it's for you."

It is Sage. I closed my eyes and tried to swallow the large amount of saliva that collected in my mouth. I patted my face, trying to warm it up.

"Hello?" I said, practically blowing a spit bubble.

"George Blandford?" This voice didn't sound a thing like Sage's, but I was so sure it was hers that it confused me.

"Is that you, Sage?" I asked. "Do you have a cold?"

"No, this is Harold Donaldson, from over at the *Gazette,* and I'm fine."

"Oh, Mr. Donaldson," I said, my breath rushing out. Mr. Donaldson is sports editor for the local paper. My body went warm with relief. As warm as it could, considering I was almost frozen to death. My fingers tingled. "I expected someone else."

"Sure. Whatever," said Mr. Donaldson. "We need someone to cover the football game this Friday night at your school. Think you could do it?"

"Yeah," I said. "Sure I could, Mr. Donaldson."

"I'll expect the article on my desk first thing Saturday morning."

"Yes, sir. Anything else?"

"Yeah, do a good job."

"Okay. Goodbye."

"Hmm hmm." There was a click, and I knew he'd hung up.

Wow, I thought. *My first real writing job.* The excitement of the whole thing gave me the courage to call Sage. I dialed her number.

"Hello?" It was Morgan.

I tried to disguise my voice. "Aach. Eez Saje Ollyfer at dis hom?"

"Hi, George," Morgan said. "Why do you want to talk to my sister?"

I rolled my eyes. How did the kid recognize my voice? "To see if she'll run away with me so we can get married. Then you can have her room."

"Well," Morgan said. "She might marry you. She's always talking about you at dinner. But I don't think Mom would like that. . . ."

All at once I was interested in what the sweet little guy had to say. "She talks about me at dinner?"

"Yeah, and that book she's writing. She wonders about your eyes and your hair and bear grease and stuff like that."

Bear grease? "Does she ever say she likes me, Morgan?"

"Better'n who? Better'n the other guys?"

Oh, Boob was resurfacing again. Haunting me as much as Angelica did. I wondered if Boob would fit in a manila envelope, too.

"Yeah," I said. "Better than the other guys. Does she like me more?"

"I'm not allowed to tell you."

"How come?"

"Sage told me she'd squish me flat if I told any guy that called how she felt. She's always talking about guys. And that book. But she talks about you the most, George."

"Are you going to tell me what she says?"

"Nope, I don't think so."

"How about getting me Sage, then?" Maybe if I pretended I really didn't want to know, Morgan would tell me.

"No, I don't want to do that, either."

"Please. With sugar on top." Sage had said that before when she was trying to get Morgan to leave the room.

"Naaah." I remembered the sugar on top thing hadn't worked.

"Hurry. This is long distance. It's costing me money."

"No, thanks," Morgan said. Then he laughed.

"Morgan, get your sister for me." I was losing patience.

"What will you do for me?" Morgan can be a real pain. Had I ever thought he was cute? No, I don't think so.

"Get her and I won't kill you the next time I visit."

"Yeah, right. You just—" There was a bunch of talking and arguing. I could hear Sage in the background, trying to get the phone from Morgan. Maybe I should walk the four houses down to her place.

"Hello?" Sage said. "Is that you, George?"

"Hi, Sage. That brother of yours is such a great kid." I only lie to Sage about Morgan. And, well, Angelica.

"I'm glad you can stand him, because some days I hate his guts," Sage said.

"I'm telling Mom," Morgan said, his voice loud. "You said you hate my guts. You said it. I heard you. And George tried to fool me. I hate you both. I hate your guts *and* your faces."

"Run and tell Mom," Sage said. "Hurry. She's not writing."

"I will!" Morgan screamed. I think his yell made me slightly deaf in my phone ear.

"Hello, George," Sage said when all was quiet.

"Hello, Sage," I said, and told her about my good luck at getting an article with what I considered a "real" paper. Sage was Sage.

"Oh, George," she said. "I'm so happy for you. I think that is terrific. Do you think they'll hire you full-time as a writer? Hey, do you think they have a fiction section for me?" I felt my eyes start to bulge; then Sage giggled. Thank goodness she was kidding. The thought of her asking for a job made my heart pound. "The newspaper is *not* where I want to get my big break. But I have heard of some writers doing that."

"No, I don't think I'll get a job full-time. I don't want one. I'll keep plugging away there while I go to the community college."

"Guess what I was doing?" Sage asked.

"Writing?"

"Yes," Sage said.

"Angelica?"

"Yes, and it's going well. Would you like me to read it to you over the phone?"

"Well . . . actually . . . I . . . I want . . ." What? What? I want to tell you what a heel I am? I want to lie to you? "I want to take you to dinner tonight. Are you free? Do you think your parents will care?"

"Mom's resting from writing, but I know she plans on doing some more tonight. She has a deadline. You know how that is, George." Sage didn't wait for me to answer. "And Daddy's still fixing teeth. I think it would be fun to go, though. There might be a problem finding a baby-sitter for Morgan. When?"

"Is seven o'clock too late?"

"It's fine," Sage said. "It's perfect. Maybe by that time Dad will be home. I'd love to. Do you mind if I bring my next few chapters?"

"No," I said. "Please bring Angelica along."

Sage giggled.

After I hung up and made arrangements with my mother to drop Sage and me off at a restaurant, I went to change into a clean shirt and pair of jeans. The only thing I could think of that would be more appropriate to wear, though, was sackcloth and ashes.

15

in the coolness
of my thoughts i see
you
walking toward me
and my breath
catches

even now
at this distance
created by memory
the warmth of it,
of you,
encircles me
and i am
snagged
tight

16

Sage

The icy-cold water rushed around Angelica's head. Once, twice, three times she went under the salty river water.

I'm going to drown, *Angelica thought, her arms slapping, her fingers clawing, grabbing, grabbing, grabbing. The last thing Angelica heard was an Indian war cry. It penetrated the air, cut through the depths, gouged into her brain.*

"301 Bears," *Angelica bubbled. Then she was unconscious. She felt her body sinking in the current and then rushing over some rapids.*

When she awoke, Angelica was propped into a sitting position next to a hot fire, wrapped in a blanket. She held a cup of cold tea.

A handsome man sat across the fire from her. He held a stick with a fish skewered on it. There was a honeycomb sitting on a cream-colored china plate nearby.

"Have some?" *the man asked, thrusting the stick at Angelica. His voice was as drippy and golden as the honey.*

"How have I come to be here?" *asked Angelica. She reached for the fish, her gloves white in the sunlight.*

"I caught you from the river," *the man said. Then he laughed. His laugh was as golden and drippy as the honey.*

One eye was covered with an eye patch made from raccoon skin.

Angelica looked past the man and noticed all of her clothing lying in the bushes. Without moving her head, she rolled her eyes down until they looked under the blanket that was wrapped around her beautifully slender body.

"They were wet," dripped the man's voice, honeylike. "I didn't want you to catch no cold."

Angelica's eyes rolled back up to face the man. Her gloved hand touched her beautiful curls.

"Pleased to meet you," she said.

George, Morgan, and I sat in Sizzler, waiting for our meal. Morgan was close to George, right under his elbow. My father wouldn't be home until late. And Mom did have that deadline.

"It's Wednesday night," Dad had reminded me when I called him at work. "You know I always stay late on Wednesday nights." This was his contribution to America's working class, a night when anyone could come in and get their teeth drilled and not miss time from their jobs. "Hope you can find a baby-sitter, but if not, have fun."

So we were having fun. All three of us.

If you ask me, the steak smell of Sizzler made a perfect background for my western story, even if my baby brother sat tucked into the ribs of the man of my dreams.

I sure wish I could incorporate smells into my novel. I think it would be great to catch a whiff of the outdoorsy-ness that is so thick in my writing. You know, things like steak cooking, and the smells from the all-you-can-eat salad bar.

Angelica and the Seminole Indians was next to my water glass. Morgan rolled his eyes this way and that. I was choked up from the drowning scene. I had cried while I wrote the part about Angelica going under the water.

"Doesn't lovey-dovey stuff make you sick?" Morgan asked George, looking up at him.

George nodded.

"Hey," Morgan said in a loud voice. "I can see right up your nose. There's hair up there, and it's black-looking, and I see something else, too. Maybe it's a booger. Wow, is it ever neat. Have you ever seen up George's nose, Sage?"

I ignored Morgan.

"Great." George's face went pink. He covered his nose with one hand and with the other tried to wipe his upper lip. I'd never seen him act so nervous. I knew it couldn't be the nose comment. Morgan always says stuff like that when we're together. Something else bothered George. Not even before major exams in school did George act this nervous. In fact, he loves taking tests. Not me. I get so nervous my stomach hurts and I'm sure I'll throw up until the moment I hand in the test.

"Sage?" George said.

"Yes?" I had ordered tea with my dinner tonight. Too bad honeycomb was not on the menu.

George took his glasses off and polished them. He cleared his throat. He wiped his upper lip. Even nervous, George was the handsomest guy in our school.

"I have something to tell you, Sage." He sipped from his water glass. He brushed his hand over the hair that stuck up. He closed his eyes and covered his face with both hands.

"How come you're sweating, George?" Morgan

85

asked. He played with his root beer, blowing bubbles, sucking the drink up the straw, then capping it with his finger.

"Am I sweating?" George asked.

"What?" I asked. "What do you want to tell me?"

"It's bad news," he said, his voice muffled.

All of a sudden I felt frightened. George had never acted this way before except once. When George was ten, his guinea pig, Delbert, died. George sat in the garage holding his dead pet because he couldn't stand to bury him. Finally Mr. Blandford came in and pried Delbert out of George's hands, then buried him out in the backyard. George never cried that I know of. But he wore the same expression then as he wore now.

"What's happened, George? Tell me, what's happened? Has somebody passed away?" It didn't make sense that we would be in a restaurant if someone had, but it was the only thing I could think of that would explain George's expression.

"Wow," said Morgan. "Somebody's died." He made his fingers into guns and rat-ta-tat-tatted them. "Aaagh," he said, clutching his chest. "I'm dying." He fell against George and drew his last breath with quite a few jerks and shakes.

"IlostAngelicaandtheSeminoleIndians." It was one big word. George looked up at me, his face stricken. "Oh, Sage, I know how important this contest is to you. And now look what I've done. Ruined your chances at fame. I know how hard this will be, now that all those chapters are gone." George's voice slipped into nothing.

I sat silent. Something in my chest grew fat and began to warm up. Never had I felt such love. How dear a dear was my dear George. Did he know that? Did he know how good he was? I felt another poem surfacing.

My dear one
My dear, dear one
you are the one
the only one dear
dear one

"It's okay," I said, touching his hand. "I had Mom put that first part into the computer for me. She can type and watch television, so she doesn't even know what she's writing."

"But," George said. "But you have it written out by hand. All the pages you've read to me have been done by hand."

I grinned at George. "I know. That's how my ideas come to me best and fastest. On this pink lined paper. And when I use the purple pen, I really get creative. Have you noticed most of the writing has been in purple ink?"

George nodded.

"So later I type it all in myself. Mom doesn't have time anymore, with this book she's doing. I sure am glad we have more than one computer, or I'd never have a chance to write."

George nodded again.

"You know the best thing of all, George?" I wanted to say, "You're the best thing of all, Man o' My Dreams." But I didn't.

He shook his head.

I bit my tongue on my George thought and forced myself to think of Angelica.

"The best part is that I don't even have to revise. Every word for Angelica is perfect."

Even bug-eyed, George was handsome.

17
George

I GUESS I SHOULD HAVE KNOWN THAT Sage would be saving her most prized possession on the computer. All her English assignments were typed. And why in the world had I thought that my disposing of Angelica would stop Sage from entering the school writing contest, anyway? Sage is not a quitter. She works hard at everything she does. This book was proof enough of that. And if I were to blow up her entire computer to get rid of Angelica, I knew there'd be another copy, bronzed or something, waiting on the living room mantel, to become number one on *The New York Times* bestseller list.

Dinner went down my throat like dry bread. Sometimes it caught at the back of my mouth and I'd have to swallow three or four times to get it to travel to my stomach, where steak and a good portion of the all-you-can-eat buffet salad bar sat like a heavy lump. I envisioned my Adam's apple going up and down and up and down as if its only purpose in life were to show dinner its destination. I wasn't hungry, but I tortured myself with every bite of food. I felt miserable. Even Morgan couldn't joke me out of my mood with all his nose, booger, and dying comments.

Sage had Angelica on the computer.

I couldn't save either one of them now.

On Friday night I picked Sage up, my notepad and pencil in hand. She was dressed in a thick navy-blue sweater and a pair of faded Levi's. She wore a navy knit cap on her head, pulled low over her ears. She'd even thought to bring a Schoolcraft blanket to wrap around herself.

It was cold. The game lights were bright against the winter sky. Bob Taylor and the rest of the players ran out onto the field, and our group of kids let out a great roar. We have a lot of school spirit, even if our players don't have a lot of skill.

Sage and I sat high on the bleachers until the icy night wind drove us down to lower seats. We huddled together, drinking hot chocolate Sage had brought from home. I took notes, trying to make the game come to life for the soon-to-be readers of *The Kalamazoo Gazette.* But how much life can you give to an article when the final score is 49–3 and the home team is the loser? The most interesting parts of the game were the times Bob Taylor blew kisses to Sage. I was pretty sure Mr. Donaldson wouldn't want to read about that kind of stuff.

"I wonder why Bob keeps gesturing to you?" I said.

"Oh, George. He thinks he likes me."

"Can you blame him? I'm not blaming him. But does he have to act so . . . dumb?"

"That's not dumb," Sage said. "It's romantic."

Bob sat on the bench, waiting for our offense's turn on the field. He clapped and called words of encouragement to our defense. Every once in a while he would look up at Sage and wave. Once he even grabbed a megaphone from a cheerleader and shouted, "Sage Oliver, will you marry me?"

She laughed and nodded. Bob bowed to us, then tossed the megaphone back to the cheerleader and, after a few minutes, ran onto the field with the team. On his way he blew another kiss at Sage. I hoped he would trip, but he was too athletic for that. And as much as I prayed for him to get hit, he survived the entire game with nothing more than a few tumbles on the ground. He is definitely an agile wide receiver.

Watching Bob make goo-goo eyes at Sage gave me the energy to stay up late and write the article for Mr. Donaldson.

Watching Bob make goo-goo eyes at Sage also kept me up later than I wanted, past finishing the article. Thanks to Boob, I was able to worry about Sage and Angelica some more.

It was during all the worrying that it hit me: There really was nothing I could do to save Sage. All my worry had been for nothing. The teachers would *not* pick her book. How could they? It was horribly written. Granted, most of the stuff turned in to the contest was horribly written. Angelica, though, was horribly-er.

So Sage had everything on the computer. So she turned in her novel Friday morning. So, sew buttons on your underwear.

Where had that come from?

I was too tired to worry anymore. I had to go to sleep.

Monday was chilly. Snow clouds piled up gray in the sky, then spilled out over our little town. By second period, snow was falling, dusting the trees and the cars in the parking lots like powdered sugar on a cake. It melted on the sidewalks.

I stared out the window in current affairs, thinking about Sage. Then, like magic, she was outside my classroom, looking in at me.

"Sage," I said, under my breath. My heart thumped at the sight of her.

She wore a long forest-green coat. Her light-colored hair hung loose and curly down her back. She motioned to me with one gloved hand, then stuck her tongue out. Not at me, but at the chance of catching a snowflake. She twirled, holding her books to her chest with one arm. She almost danced in the cold afternoon air. It was like watching a slow-motion movie, the way she moved, her hair waving out from her body, her free arm extended. She motioned to me again, to come outside with her, and I stood, forgetting where I was, only thinking of being with her.

"Mr. Blandford," said Coach Van Slyke. Coach Van Slyke always jokes that the reason Schoolcraft High School doesn't have a winning football team is because his attentions are divided. He is a thought-provoking teacher, though, even if our football team is 0 and 8 this year. This is not unusual. We've lost in football for as long as I can remember. And our latest score, 49–3, has not been our worst.

There's something about the Greyhound fans. They keep plugging away and cheering for their team. We all have that wonderful team spirit. And anyway, our basketball players are better. It is rumored that many years ago Schoolcraft produced a winning basketball team. Our principal still talks about the seasons they won. But Mr. Kaufman is old, and I think it happened when he was going to school here himself.

"Mr. Blandford," the coach said again. "Although the beauties of the unexpected snow are waiting for you, please remain seated until class is over."

I grinned at Coach Van Slyke and sat back down. Bob Taylor, who sits catty-corner from me, groaned and rolled his eyes toward the ceiling. A few kids in the room laughed. When I looked back out the window, Sage was gone.

18

```
s
 w
  i
   r         t
    l       w
             i
              r         d
               l       o
                      w
                     n
              hold on to the air
           ride down on the air
         to me,
```

delighted.

s n a t c h   c a t c h
your way
here to me
awaiting your arrival
the delivery,

amazing.

P   e   d   e
 r c   a c
  an   n

to melt
cool on my face
and bare wrists,

exquisite.

19
Sage

CHERI WALKED ME HOME BECAUSE TODAY SHE WAS free of a man and my man was working late on the school newspaper.

"I can't believe you've known about him all this time and you never told me," she said.

Snow was piled up on the lawns and sidewalk. The air was biting cold.

"Cheri," I said. "You've known about Andrew for years."

Cheri looked at me, her face a blank. "No, I haven't. I don't think I've ever seen him before."

"Yes, you have." I pulled my coat a little closer. "He and George have been friends a long time. They're always together."

"They're not always together. Anytime I see George he's with you."

I thought about this a second. It's true that George and I have been seeing more and more of each other. The thought made my stomach tighten into an excited ball. "Well, they used to be together all the time. And they run track and do the newspaper, too."

Cheri's face looked like she'd never even seen George, much less knew he and Andrew were friends.

"He's my worst enemy," I said.

"Andrew?" Cheri's voice rose along with her eyebrows.

"Yeah, the guy who—"

"The guy who snorts when he laughs?" Cheri asked.

"Yep, he's the one."

"No way. Sage, I tell you right here and now that Andrew has yet to snort in front of me."

"You just haven't noticed. He snorted when I read to all of you in the library."

"I'll have to keep an ear out for that. Anyway, I like this guy."

"You like every guy," I said.

"True. But not this way. This one is different."

"You always say that."

"Do I?"

I laughed and stopped on the sidewalk. The wind blew a little snow from the branches of a tree down onto us. I love the snow. I'd have to have a winter scene in my Angelica book. Snow, warm fires and hot chocolate can be so romantic. But first things first.

"Are you in love, Cheri?"

"No," she said, glancing at me from beneath her brown bangs. "But I am in like. A nice kind of like."

"A long-lasting kind of like?" I asked.

"Maybe," she said with a shrug.

We were at my house now. Cheri only had a couple more blocks to go until she was home. We separated, and I went in to add my friend's feelings to a few scenes of my newest book.

"It was so strange, George," I said.

George and I sat in my kitchen at the counter, sipping hot chocolate piled high with whipped cream. It was Thanksgiving weekend, finally. No school for four days. One day for parades, football games, and visiting relatives. Then I would be able to write to my heart's content.

Morgan hid somewhere close by, probably in a drawer. I ignored him.

"As soon as I set *Angelica and the Seminole Indians* in the contest box a week ago, I got the distinct feeling that I was going to win. Goose bumps all up and down my arms. Did you know I ended up with thirty-six chapters? Can you believe it? Thirty-six chapters and I felt like I could write on and on."

George smiled. His hair was wet because I'd insisted that we walk around the park during the storm for a while. I hoped it would snow the whole Thanksgiving holiday.

"Thirty-six chapters, huh?" George asked. "How did you end it?"

"I can't tell you that. If I do, you won't be surprised. But I can let you in on one little secret." I leaned toward George and then whispered, "There's going to be a sequel."

George laughed.

A funny feeling bubbled around in my heart area. It kind of reminded me of a description Cheri had given me of a kiss from her best-kissing boyfriend. "The feeling was like soda pop—you know when you've drunk too much? And you get that bubbly sensation?"

"I thought you burped," I'd said, and Cheri and I had laughed.

I needed to switch the conversation around now. This feeling was too close to what Cheri had described.

"Did you turn anything in?" I asked George. "To the contest, I mean?"

He nodded.

"What?"

"I can't tell you that. If I do, you won't be surprised."

"Oh, George," I said.

"Oh, Sage."

We looked at each other a long time. It was what Angelica would have called a deep look. A look of feeling. A look of passion. The bubbles were back. It felt like I'd been drinking soda pop for a week.

George took off his glasses and rubbed them on his damp sweater. There was fuzz on one of the lenses when he looked back at me. "I want to kiss you," he said.

My stomach leaped a little.

"Gross," said a voice from the broom closet.

"Ignore him," George said. "I'm sure he'll see us kiss again."

"Go ahead," I told him. "What's taken you so long, anyway?

"I thought you were waiting for your dream man to come along." His breath was warm on my cheek. Then ever so lightly, not even a kiss, really, George's lips brushed mine. My hair fell forward as I leaned over the hot-chocolate cups to get closer to him.

"Sage," Mom's voice echoed in the foyer. Morgan stepped out of the broom closet and ran to meet her.

"I'm telling," he said as he went past. "You two were kissing. Mom, they were kissing." Morgan made throw-up noises as he ran.

George jumped to his feet, knocking his stool onto the kitchen floor.

"We're in the kitchen, Mom." My voice sounded funny to my ears, like I was talking down a long tube, or was far away.

"I gotta go," George said, righting the stool, then putting the half-filled hot-chocolate cup into the sink.

"It's okay," I said. "You can kiss me. I'm fifteen."

"I know that," he said.

I could hear Mom walking down the tiled hall, coming closer to the kitchen, her feet shuffling. Morgan talked nonstop as they made their way to where we were.

"And then I peeked out of the closet," he said.

"You were peeking again?" Mom asked.

"Only a little."

"I don't like it when you spy on your sister."

"But let me tell you. George is like all the rest of those weirdo guys. He's a kisser, too."

"I gotta go," George said again.

I got off my stool and ran over to him. Could any of the men in Angelica's life be as wonderful as he was? I was sure they could not. I grabbed hold of his arm. His cotton sweater was damp under my fingers.

"Wait," I said, and George stopped moving. He looked down at me, and his eyes were even darker than our hot chocolate.

"What?"

"We were getting ready to do something."

George looked at me so hard I felt my face turn warm. He took hold of my elbows and pulled me close.

It was then that Mom and Morgan came into the kitchen.

George let go of me and stared at my mom, but still I stood near him. I glanced back at my interrupting relatives.

Mom held Morgan up on one hip. His arms were wrapped around her. Some of her blond hair was pulled back at the nape of her neck. The rest hung in straggles around her face. Her dress was a rag. Literally. I mean she really looked like she was someone from raggedy days. You know, when people wore clothing made from burlap bags, patches and all.

Somehow Mom looked better than she normally did when she dressed in costume. She looked glamorous. She looked authorish. She looked surprised. Maybe it was the moment. My moment.

"See," Morgan screeched. *He* was looking particularly weasel-like. "I told you they were kissing in the kitchen. Isn't it gross? Isn't it disgusting?"

Mom set Morgan down on the floor, where he began to fake-barf into the garbage can.

I smiled at my mother. Were her eyes sparkling? Were mine?

"Hello, George," Mom said, and I saw she had blacked out a front tooth. "I wondered if you were still here. Then Morgan came in to me. He's my little informant, you know."

I snorted. Oh, yuck. I sounded like Andrew. I wasn't sure how to take a snort back, so I let it go, hoping George didn't notice.

George still looked at Mom. He ran his tongue over

his teeth. At that moment I wanted my mother and brother out of the kitchen. I wanted George and me tangled in the most romantic kiss ever experienced. I wanted Angelica to be jealous.

"Mrs. Oliver. How's your book going?" George asked, and without waiting for her to answer, he said, "I really have to go."

"Mom." I stepped in front of George, blocking his way out of the kitchen. "Don't you think I'm old enough to kiss George? You know, seeing that I'm fifteen."

"You haven't kissed George yet?" my mother asked, sounding shocked. She pushed at her loose hair, then walked over to where I stood, her bare feet slapping at the tile floor. She put her arm around my shoulders and gave me a squeeze. "Why, I'd have thought the two of you would never have stopped after that kiss in second grade." Mother looked at George in a funny way. "Don't you like to kiss?" she asked him.

"That kiss never happened," I said, quite interested in the answer George was going to give.

George looked from me to Mom, then again at me. "Yes, Mrs. Oliver, I like to kiss. I've kissed plenty of girls." He sounded a little offended that someone might think he hadn't.

I was surprised. "You've *kissed* other girls? I didn't know that, George." But he ignored me.

Morgan began fake-barfing anew.

"You see, Sage has been . . . Sage has been waiting for the man of her dreams."

Now Mom gave *me* a funny look. I shrugged.

"George," Mom said. "Would you and your parents

please come for dinner Friday evening? I should be done with the first draft of this book."

"I think that would be great," George said, looking at everyone but me. "I'll tell them you invited us over."

"And George," Mom said. "I do give you permission to kiss Sage."

"Oh," he said. "Thanks." His eyes bugged a bit, and he sidestepped me and hurried off down the hall. I heard the door open and close. Outside, snow still fell. I wondered if I should be upset that George had kissed other girls. I decided not to be.

Mom opened her arms to me, and I hugged her, the cloth of her ragged dress rough under my fingers. Morgan leaned toward us, and Mom scooped him up and set him on the counter.

"He's the man I've been waiting for," I said. I let out a sigh.

"I've known that since you were in the second grade," Mom said.

"All this kissing stuff is making my stomach hurt. I'm not *ever* kissing any ol' girl," said Morgan. He wrinkled his nose. "Just you, Mom. Sage, will you make me some hot chocolate? I think that would make my stomach feel better."

I couldn't help laughing, my whole chest being filled with bubbles.

20

George

WHO WOULDN'T HAVE KNOWN THAT MOM and Dad would accept an invitation to eat with the Olivers? Mom's been interested in Mrs. Oliver forever. Can you blame her?

"Why do I see her in so many strange articles of clothing?" Mom always asks. My mother wouldn't be caught dead not color-coordinated. I think that has to do with her decorator background.

I have to admit that I worried whether Mrs. Oliver would be in costume or not for this meal. If she was, what would Mom say? "Your outfit doesn't quite go with this dinner"?

"Listen," I said to Mom and Dad. They watched television before we went over to Sage's house.

"Yes, dear?" That was Mom. She was absorbed in an old Lawrence Welk rerun. Usually she laughs at fabrics and color combinations she sees on the program. Dad watches to humor her. This isn't his favorite show. He likes the documentaries with monkeys best. "Get a load of that beehive," Mom said.

I checked out the screen, but all I saw was a woman with tall hair. "I was wondering if maybe you two could, well, not mention anything about what Mrs. Oliver might be wearing."

Mom turned and looked at me. "Do you think she'll be in something weird?"

Dad glanced around. They both looked expectant, like maybe, because Sage and I were friends, I might actually know why Mrs. Oliver insisted on dressing as the characters from her books.

I sighed. "She doesn't always. Only when she's writing."

"That is the strangest behavior," Mom said, shaking her head.

I had to admit that seeing Sage's mom dressed like Joan of Arc once had given me a jolt. I think it was the sword she carried when she answered the door that surprised me.

I leaned over toward Mom. "If she is weird-looking, please, let's go with it. You know, pretend we're used to this kind of stuff."

Dad lowered his glasses. "Everybody's their own kind of weird," he said, then rubbed his head like maybe he was buffing it.

Mom turned back to the television. "Son, you can count on me."

But I didn't have to count on Mom. I mean, the Olivers met us at the door that evening. Dr. Oliver wasn't wearing his dental clothes, and Mrs. Oliver was dressed like a normal person. She greeted me with a kiss, and then all the grown-ups started shaking hands.

"I'm all done with my novel," Mrs. Oliver said.

"And I'm through with teeth for a few days. Except my own," Dr. Oliver added; then he laughed. "Now for a little time to rest and relax."

Mrs. Oliver ushered us into the house with a wave of her hand.

Sage came into the foyer. Morgan followed. Sage grabbed at my arm and looked up at me. I had the incredible urge to move her hair off her face, push all those curls back, really get a good look at her.

"George," she said, her eyes sparkling. "I've got a surprise for you. Come here."

"Okay." I started after Sage, almost forgetting Mom and Dad, though I could hear the adults talking about the weather.

Morgan was quick to intercept me. "Can I go, too?"

Sage looked back. "No."

"She's gonna read something to you." Morgan rubbed at his nose with the sleeve of his shirt. "Something kissy, probably."

"You are?" I asked.

"Well." Sage glanced down at the floor. When she looked back up her whole face seemed to smile. "I *have* been working on something. But you"—she pointed to Morgan—"can't go." In the background I could hear the Olivers taking my parents to another room, probably to watch TV, if my folks had anything to do with it.

"*Is* it something kissy?" I asked.

"Come with me to Mom's office," Sage said. She held her hand out to me.

My stomach gave a jump. Writing was one thing I did not even want to think about. I took Sage's hand. It was cool, and I could feel her tiny bones beneath my fingers.

"There isn't any kissing yet," Sage said. She pushed Morgan back while she talked. "But there will be."

"Ger-oss," Morgan said, only his voice was muffled because Sage's hand covered his mouth.

Sage eyed Morgan. "In fact, there will be lots of kisses. Kisses that go on for pages."

Morgan stopped short outside Mrs. Oliver's office. "Are you going to be talking about that kind of disgusting stuff?"

"Yes," said Sage.

"I'm telling Mom."

"Okay. And let her know that the kisses also have heaving bosoms thrown in."

"What?" I asked. Heaving bosoms and kisses?

Morgan gasped in a big breath of air. "You said *bosoms*." His voice was low. "Now you are in *huge* trouble." He took off at a run, screaming for his mother as he went.

"Bosoms really can make him move," Sage said with a laugh.

"I can't blame him," I said.

"Oh, George," Sage said. She went into the office and fumbled through a stack of pink paper. She shook out a page and, smiling a gentle smile, began to read.

Cherilena could not keep her space-suit mask on. Irregardless of the dangers that it meant for her to remove it, remove it she did. And with a passion the one-eyed spaceman had never seen before in all his space travels.

"Glork," he garbled, which translated means, "There are dangers here only you can discover, Hot-Lipped One."

But Cherilena knew now that there was only one thing left for her to do. It was to kiss the man of her dreams, the one-eyed man of her dreams. Yes, she had wanted to fly the Enterprise *herself. Yes, she had wanted to tame the planet Zevlo's snake-things. Yes, she had wanted to fight off the invaders of Sharsnon, her very own planet that had given her life.*

But none of that was to come to pass. No, none of that would ever be now. Because Cherilena knew what true love was. And what it wasn't. It wasn't flying starships, it wasn't taming snake-things. It wasn't invaders.

Love was the one-eyed man with the shiny metallic eye patch. Love was good. Love wasn't bad.

Yes, love was good.

So very, very, very good.

I looked at Sage, then cleared my throat. "Is it time to eat?"

"Well?" she asked.

"Dinner?" I said.

"What did you think?"

"Is it turkey?"

"No, it's the planet Sharsnon."

"I mean leftovers."

"You're not answering me, George."

I fumbled with the buttons on my shirt. Angelica was gone, and in her place stood Cherilena, Spacewoman from Writer's Hell. I didn't know what to say. "I don't know what to say," I said.

Sage moved up close to me. "Tell me what you like best."

This I could do. "I like you best, Sage." And I meant every word.

"What did you like about my new book?"

"I liked . . ." I racked my brain, but it seemed the only things I could remember were a one-eyed spaceman who garbled his words in a strange language, and the word *irregardless*. I tried again. "I liked . . ."

"Dinner!" Dr. Oliver called. "Sage, George. We're waiting for you."

"We better hurry," I said, smacking my hands together.

During dinner I found out one more thing to add to my writer's burden. It was right when I had taken Sage's hand in mine (under the table so no parents would see) and had just taken a bite of roasted pheasant. Sage was talking, and I only half-listened to her words. Mostly I thought how nice her hand felt in mine. In the back of my mind I heard:

". . . and so I don't really have a chance. Not with George entering. He'll win for sure."

Everybody at the table looked at me.

I started to tune in. "What?"

"You entered?" Mom asked.

That contest, back to haunt me again. And this time from my own mother. I nodded.

"What did you write, George?" This was Mrs. Oliver.

"Nothing really," I said.

"Don't be so shy, George," Sage said. "You know what a good writer you are. I bet you do win. I won't, not with you against me."

She looked at me then, right in the eyes, and that's what did me in. I could never be against Sage Oliver. Now, not only did I have to worry about her story being in the contest, I was going to have to worry about competing with her.

There was only one thing to do.

Get my work out of the contest.

"Ms. Chapin, you do not know who dis iz?"

"Excuse me?"

"Dis iz goot."

"Goot?"

"Not my name, goot, but goot. You mus know my definition, when all iz well?"

109

"You mean 'good'?"

"Yes, dis iz co-rect. I mus warn you to change de tings you will see."

"I think you must have the wrong number."

"No. No mis-take. And I call so no mis-take will continue. Der iz a stoo-dent, one George Blandford. He haz entered ze writing contest."

"George Blandford?"

"But yes, zen you know of heem?"

"George?"

"Hiz entry to dis contest must be withdrawn as soon as poss-e-bull."

"Oh?"

"And der iz more dat I must tell you."

"Is there?"

"You are so goot to tawk like dis wiff me."

"Do you happen to know what time it is?"

"Early."

"Two-thirty in the morning."

"In my country dis time iz not so early. We rise wit de birds or some-ting. So you weel diz-miss George Blandford's entry?"

"I'll dismiss George, period. I do have Caller ID, Mr. Blandford. And I'll be seeing you Monday morning."

"Wait, Ms. Chapin. This is really important." The accent was gone.

And so was Ms. Chapin.

I hung up the phone and walked in slow motion back to bed. I might just as well enjoy my last few hours. I'd be a dead man come Monday morning.

21

I
Search
For who I am
Then find
that when I'm with you
I know the
answer

22
Sage

"YOU MEAN YOU BASED THAT CHARACTER ON ME?"
Cheri's voice was full of admiration.

"Can you think of a better person?" I asked. I
straightened the stack of pink paper, tapping it on the
edge of the desk in my room.

Cheri bowed her head. "I'm honored." She lounged
on my bed. "I just hope I can live up to what you're
talking about in there."

"Live up to it? Good grief, you're my inspiration."

"I guess I should stop talking to you so much." Cheri
smiled at me.

I grinned back. "Mom told me her friends and ene-
mies always end up in her work. Remember that one
scene I read to you from the book *Herrington Carter*?"

"You mean the one with the good-looking guy who
fights the squid things in all that relish stuff?"

"That's the one."

"I remember," Cheri said. "What a great scene." She
gave a sigh.

I had to agree. That Herrington character in Mom's
book is great. Talk about a wonderful lover. "Well," I

continued, "the squid dealie was based on Dad's boss at the college."

"No way," Cheri said.

"Yeah, it's true. In fact, if you were to meet him, then read the part again, you'd see the resemblance. Mom's pretty good at that. You know, making strange characters seem real. Or making strange people into true characters."

"So are you, Sage. I love your writing." Cheri sighed again.

I felt a blush creep up my cheeks. I worry that maybe I'll never be able to take a compliment about my writing without turning red.

Cheri plopped onto my pillow and crossed her hands under her head.

"Tell me how things are going with you and Andrew." I have to admit seeing Andrew with Cheri has made him more likable to me. Not that he had stopped that obnoxious snorting or toned down his loud and offending laugh. I guess it's the way he looks at Cheri that changed my feelings about him. It's obvious that the two of them like each other. And anyone who likes Cheri, who has been my best friend almost since the day I could walk, is a friend of mine. Even if he is a Thieving White Man.

"Pretty good. He told me George entered the contest."

"Yep, he did." The thought of George and me in a contest together seemed so romantic. And it would work great in my newest novel. A competition between Cherilena and her spaceman friend.

"What did he enter?"

I shrugged. "I think a few short stories. He's a good writer, Cheri. I don't stand a chance now that he's in there."

"Andrew's done some stuff also."

I rolled my eyes, but not where Cheri could see me.

"He read a little to me," Cheri said.

"Oh yeah? What was it about?"

"They were stories or something." Cheri sat up and swung her legs over the edge of the bed. "All this introspective stuff."

I nodded and slipped chapter five of *Cherilena: Woman Conqueror of the Wide Squadron Galaxy* into its folder.

"If you promise not to mention this, I'll tell you something," Cheri said.

"What?"

"Your stuff is much better."

That night, after the sun sank behind the evergreen trees that edged our property, I climbed into bed, dressed in my red thermal underwear, with Cherilena in a pile beside me and some green lined paper. I had a whole hour to create. Tomorrow at school, they would announce who had won the contest. It felt like a thousand butterflies filled my stomach. They batted around leftover Thanksgiving dinner.

The clock on my beside table said 10:35, but I picked up the phone and called George anyway.

He answered on the fourth ring.

"George," I said. "What are you doing?"

"I was thinking, Sage."

"About the contest?"

George was quiet a moment. "Kind of," he said.

"Mostly I was thinking about seeing Ms. Chapin in the morning."

"Do you have an appointment with her?"

"You could say that." George didn't sound very happy.

"Well, I couldn't sleep," I said. "I wanted to talk to you for a minute."

"All right. I probably won't be good phone company, but I'll try. I'm a little worried about tomorrow."

"Me too." It's amazing how similar George and I are. Like two peas in a pod. Both of us nervous about what Ms. Chapin would say.

We talked for a few minutes. Then I was struck with a writing idea: Cherilena battling a bog-type creature. A bog-type creature similar to Ms. Chapin, with a nasty disposition and the need to lecture.

"Good luck tomorrow, George," I said. "At your meeting and in the contest, too."

George groaned. "I sure as heck am gonna need it," he said.

"Not you, George. Your writing is great."

"I'm not so sure good writing is going to save me."

"Oh, yes it will," I said, squishing my shoulders into my pillow and settling back in a comfortable position. When George and I are married I'll call him on the phone every day he goes to work. Usually he's great to talk to. In fact, I enjoy just hearing him breathe, which was what was happening now.

23
George

MONDAY MORNING CAME TOO SOON. All I could think was how Ms. Chapin had sounded when she said she'd see me at school. The memory made it hard for me to swallow.

I made my way, in slow motion, down the corridor toward Ms. Chapin's class, where I would meet her. The closer I got to her room, the slower I walked.

"What is wrong with me?" I whispered to the high ceiling of the hall. Early-morning light slipped in through the windows. Outside, the sky was gray with coming snow. "Everyone and his dog has Caller ID. Why didn't I think of that?"

I was just outside her classroom now. Taking a deep breath, I peeked through the glass in the door. Ms. Chapin sat at her desk, looking through a stack of papers. I knocked. Glancing up, she nodded for me to come in.

"Mr. Blandford," she said, and motioned for me to sit.

"I guess I should explain . . . ," I started.

"You're lucky I'm in such a good mood."

Good mood? Her face sure didn't show it. "I'm glad about that," I said, and cleared my throat. "You see, I was worried about being in the contest with other people."

Ms. Chapin raised her eyebrows.

"What I mean is, I'm not that competitive. Not really. And, well, I had changed my mind about challenging other writers."

"Not to worry, Mr. Blandford, because I don't remember seeing your submission."

"That's the thing," I said.

"The thing?" she said, her voice sarcastic. "Tell me the title of your entry."

Okay, here it was, right now, the moment I had not been waiting for. "I'd rather not."

Ms. Chapin shifted in her seat. "I see."

I pulled at the already loose collar of my sweatshirt with my finger. "Well, I'm not sure you do. There are some things I don't want people to know about me. And my submission is, er, one of them."

Ms. Chapin leaned forward, resting both palms flat on her desk. "Let's not start the day in such a way," she said. "You're trying my patience. Let it suffice to say, Mr. Blandford, that your entry never made its way across my desk for the final reading. It must have been cut before it ever got to me. You didn't win."

"I didn't?" Relief seemed to flood me to my fingertips. A flash of disappointment followed. "Oh."

"Now the phone call. George, I'd rather no prank calls be made to my home."

"I'm sorry," I said, nodding. "It'll never happen again."

"See that it doesn't. Is there anything else you need to tell me?"

The disappointment of losing was really sinking in now. "No."

"Then you're dismissed. See you in class."

I stood and walked from the room, my face burning. I had *lost.*

"I lost," I said to nobody as I made my way to my locker. The hall was filling up with people. School would be starting soon.

"It's good that I lost," I mumbled to myself. "But it's also embarrassing." I'd kind of thought I might win that twenty bucks from Andrew. I had *wanted* to win that twenty bucks.

At my locker I stopped to think. This really was a good thing. If *I* hadn't even placed, then Sage didn't have a chance, either. But what would she do when she found out?

"Oh, no," I said, digging through my books to get the things I'd need for the day. "This is just great."

How could such a simple contest prove so hard for me? Everything was so topsy-turvy. Sage wouldn't win, but she wanted to. She couldn't win, and I felt awful for her.

I imagined, in at least a hundred different ways, Sage's reaction to not winning first place.

Imagination # 1: "George," Sage said, her green eyes filling with tears, "they didn't choose *Angelica and the Seminole Indians.*" A lone tear would fall from one very beautiful eye, catching for a moment on her lashes. In my imagination, I would wipe the tear away gently, carefully. Then I would kiss her.

Imagination #2: Sage would swear vengeance on Ms. Chapin and the rest of the judging faculty, and I would talk her out of doing something dreadful. Then I would kiss her.

Imagination #3: Sage would weep openly in the hall. When Bob Taylor came to comfort her, I would punch him square in the jaw, knocking him unconscious. With a wide, sweeping motion, I would pull Sage close to my chest. Then I would kiss her.

Imagination #4: Sage would leap to her feet after hearing the winners' names and run from the school, crying with great sobs. I would follow behind her, stopping her just before she ran into the street in front of a large UPS truck. Then I would kiss her.

In all my imaginings, I wore contacts.

And, frighteningly enough, all my imaginings sounded like Sage had written them.

I spent Monday morning the way I always do, waiting in the newsroom. One of my jobs is to make sure the school paper gets printed and is ready for distribution.

Andrew flopped down next to me on the beat-up sofa. "I entered the contest," he said.

"You've told me that a thousand times," I said.

"Well, did you?"

"I've told you that a thousand times, too."

I glanced at Andrew. He wanted something, I could tell by looking at his face. "What?" I asked.

"And Sage?" Andrew asked.

I rolled my eyes. "Why don't you like her?" I asked. "Why is it that you and she don't like each other?"

"Her writing?" Andrew said, like he was asking me a question.

"No, I mean it. Be serious. This is one time I could have used your help and support. This has been really hard on me. But all you've done is snort, Darby."

Andrew took a moment to answer. "You really mean that, don't you, Blandford?"

"Yeah, I do. This thing has been giving me nightmares."

I waited for the snort, but it didn't come.

"Hey, I didn't know. I thought you were kidding. I was just playing along."

I dropped my head into my hands and said nothing.

"And I like Sage fine. She doesn't like me—I think because there have been times I've kept the two of you apart."

"Darby," I said, my voice cracking. Not because I was going to cry, but because this had been such a strain. "What'll I do? Sage won't win that contest. She can't. Angelica is ridiculous. It's so awful it's hilarious. She's going to be heartbroken."

"Hey, guys." It was one of the freshman reporters. "Ms. Chapin told me to tell you the papers are done."

"All right," I said, and let out a big sigh. "We're out of here, Darby."

"Your look, it covers me," Andrew said. "And makes me whole, it fills my heart, completes my soul. Your breath, it soothes me. . . ."

"Wait," I said. "How do you know that?"

Andrew grinned at me. "You turned it in to class last year, in English, remember? I memorized it, thought it was pretty good. I'll have you know it worked for me. I used it on Cheri."

"You're kidding. That's how you got Cheri to like you?"

"Well, that was the beginning of it all. My charm won her over." Andrew leaned close to me. "Sage is a romantic, Blandford. Soothe her with your words. Think about it."

"Papers," someone called and Andrew and I were off. He'd left me thinking. By my last class my head pounded.

When sixth period arrived, I got permission to leave class so I could take some Advil. I didn't go back. Instead, I went and stood by the ceramics room, where I knew Sage was. I peeked through the glass at her. She sat behind a potter's wheel, covered with a spattered shirt that hung long over her clothing. Her hair was pulled back in a braid, but curls had escaped their trap and hung loose near her face. She was intent on what she was doing, molding the spinning clay in front of her, lengthening and fattening it with her small hands. Someone must have called her name because Sage looked up, and after a moment threw her head back and laughed.

"Oh, Sage," I said. "Your look, it covers me, and makes me whole, it fills my heart, completes my soul." I closed my eyes and breathed in a big breath, trying to remember Sage, her smiles and pouts and the almost-taste of her lips. The memory of Sage was as sweet as she was.

Opening my eyes, I watched her for the better part of a half hour. I watched her laugh and then bend, concentrated, over her work. At last she was satisfied with her pottery. She stopped the wheel and stood back, looking at her work. A couple of girls came and stood near her; then the teacher, Mr. Weston, came by and nodded his approval. With a wire, Sage removed her pottery. She put it on a brick and set it on a shelf full of other things that needed to be fired.

And then the announcements began. I saw her lift her hands, a little grimy, to her face.

The gesture almost broke my heart. "I can't stay, Sage," I said. "I just can't." A knot came up in my throat. After all my imaginings, after all the Sage-saving I had done in my mind, I turned away and walked back to my own classroom to collect my books and coat. I couldn't bear to see Sage hurt after watching her so happy and carefree.

"Hey, Blandford, wait up." It was Andrew's voice, but I didn't stop. I pushed the door open and started outside, across the common area.

"Hey, I'm here for ya," Andrew called. He had followed me. A heavy snow fell. It covered tables and benches, inches thick. It decorated the bare trees and waist-high bushes. I looked back behind Andrew and saw Cheri, waiting for him near the door.

Andrew caught up to me.

"I can't watch Sage be hurt," I said.

He didn't say anything, but reached out and smacked me on the back.

"I'm going on home," I said. "Cheri's waiting for you."

A lightweight blanket of new snow covered the dirty tramped-on snow of the morning. I crunched through it.

"It's gonna be all right, Blandford," Andrew said.

"You don't know," I said. "This was so important to her."

"If I didn't know better, I'd think you're really in love."

I shook my head. "Go on back to Cheri, Darby. She's probably cold."

Andrew turned away and walked toward Cheri. Together they went into the building.

I tried not to listen to the announcements, but they echoed through the commons, muffled only a little by the swirling snow. I stuck my shaking hands deep into my pockets and pulled my shoulders forward in a slump.

Should I stay or should I go?

I couldn't make the decision, and I also couldn't seem to make my feet move. I stood, almost frozen, all alone until I heard Ms. Chapin's voice come over the intercom. I was healed! Now I could move.

I ran back inside and slumped against the wall, closing my eyes.

"This year," Ms. Chapin said, and I could see her in my mind, her hair cut close to her head, her cold eyes, "we, the English teachers here at Schoolcraft High School, had a tough decision to make." Sarcasm seemed to drip from the intercom.

"Many of the entries were well presented. Clever, witty, touching." Ms. Chapin's voice wasn't sounding so sarcastic after all. "In fact, deciding was so tough, we have chosen two first-place winners. But let's talk about the third-place finalist, Rick Walton, for his collection of rhyming picture books. Second-place finalist is last year's winner, Andrew Darby, for his *I am I* essays. And the two first-place winners—drumroll, please . . ." There was silence for a moment. Then somebody in the office pushed on a recording of a drummer's roll. ". . . an anonymous contribution of poems entitled *From My Heart* and the hilarious parody *Angelica and the Seminole Indians* by Sage Oliver."

A scream that sounded like it came from a terrified woman echoed around the hall. It bounced off the ceiling and the lockers and smacked me in the face.

Who's screaming? I thought, confused. *And why don't they shut up?*

I spun around, nearly falling in the snow that had melted from my shoes. Was it Cheri because Andrew had won again?

Then I realized I was the screamer.

Sage had won.

24

You are my summer,
in this winter of our lives.
Warm me with your smiles,
set our season on fire.

25
Sage

I STOOD WITH MY BOOKS PRESSING AGAINST MY chest. Janet Schaertl and Wendy Rogers were jumping up and down. Classmates gathered around.

"You've won, Sage!" Janet shouted. "I can't believe it. Who are you taking with you to T.G.I. Friday's? Bob Taylor? You are so lucky!"

My smile felt frozen to my face. I answered questions as they were asked, but I could hardly remember who spoke to me. All I knew was that I had won. *Angelica and the Seminole Indians* had been chosen as the first-place winner.

I had to find George. I had to find him right then. But I couldn't break away. People were everywhere. Bob Taylor came into the hall and pushed his way through the few girls that remained, and then stood there, grinning. Friends and acquaintances hollered their congratulations. Soon the hall was empty of every-one except Bob and me.

My mind felt like it was full of cotton. I didn't think I'd be able to swallow.

"Sage," Bob said, breathing out my name. "I didn't know you were a writer." He put one hand on the back of my head and smoothed my braid. "And what a funny title! Angelica and what? Indians?" He leaned close, laughing. "Did you think you'd win?"

I looked up at him. His face was . . . well . . . merry. Happy. Getting closer to mine.

The double door at the end of the corridor opened and closed. I heard someone's tennis shoes, wet from the snow, squeaking toward us.

Bob's mouth loomed close to me.

"Leave me alone," I said.

"Sage, Sage, Sage," he said. His breath smelled like that afternoon's tacos. "You know you want this. Every girl in this school wants to be kissed by me."

"You stuck-up jerk." George's voice was hot with anger.

I looked over at him. His hand was on Bob's shoulder.

"George," I said.

"This is between Sage and me, Blandford. Get the hell out of here."

"George," I said again.

Bob turned from me and, without warning, punched George right in the jaw. George stepped back three times and fell against the lockers. His books scattered across the floor. Bob turned to face me again. I could tell he was angry even though he smiled.

"Where was I?" he said between gritted teeth.

"How dare you? How dare you hit anyone at all, especially my best friend? Who do you think you are?"

I slapped Bob, hard, across the face.

"You little . . ." Bob loomed close for a moment, towering over me. Then he turned and started down the corridor. "You are such an ass," he said, jabbing his finger at George. I thought Bob might hit George again, but he didn't. He slammed out the door, yelling how it was no wonder I'd never been kissed and that it wouldn't be long before the entire school knew there was something wrong with me because I didn't like kissing.

George laughed out loud.

"George," I said, running over to where he was picking up his books. I knelt beside him to help.

"Sage," he said. "My only opportunity to be your hero and I blow it."

"Your lip. It's swelling. There's going to be a bruise on your chin."

George shrugged. "Sage, Angelica won."

I sucked my breath in. "Ms. Chapin called it hilarious. She called it a parody." My voice cracked with embarrassment. "Oh, George. Angelica was supposed to be a serious book."

George set his things down and put his arms around me. He pulled me near his chest. I rested my face against his sweater. It smelled a bit like a wet newspaper.

"A parody," I said. Then, with a small choked noise, I started to cry.

26

George

I STAYED WITH SAGE FOR A LONG time in the corridor. We sat on the floor, my arms around her, Sage crying. Her heart was broken.

"I worked so hard on Angelica," she said over and over again. We were still outside the ceramics room, and Mr. Weston kept looking at us. Finally he came out to see what was wrong.

"Sage?" he asked. "Are you okay?"

"I won the writing contest," was all Sage could say to him. Then she started crying rather loudly.

"Yes, I know," Mr. Weston said. He sounded confused. "Congratulations."

Sage let out a wail. I nodded a thank-you to him for her.

"Let me walk you home," I said after a while. "The janitor is due anytime."

"You're right," Sage said. She covered her face with her hands, then dropped them into her lap. "I can't cry here all week, can I? I need to do this at home." She looked at me and smiled. Her face looked puffy, and her nose was red. "I wonder who it was that tied with Angelica? I wonder if their stuff was as awful as mine?"

"I don't even have a Kleenex to offer you," I said to her.

"What high-school guy does?"

Sage was right. But I wouldn't let myself be comforted. I was a slouch of a friend. I could never be the hero Sage wanted and needed. Here she was crying over her book and I couldn't do anything except pat her on the shoulder.

To top all that, Boob Taylor punched me in the mouth and what did I do? Nothing. Absolutely nothing. My face turned red from the embarrassment of remembering Sage hitting him back.

"What's wrong?" She sniffed. "Do you have a fever or something?"

I could only pray for a fever. I gathered my things, and we went outside. The snow had stopped.

"In this weather, who knows?" I said. "It could be the flu." But I knew. I blushed the true color of any coward. I was so upset at failing Sage that I didn't even hear what she said. I only noticed that she had stopped talking. She gave me an unhappy look.

"Excuse me?" I asked.

"George. Please, listen to me. This is important."

I felt my face begin to redden again. We were at the corner now. The snow was trampled on the sidewalk. Evergreens that edged the lawn pushed in at us. The least I could do was hold the branches away for her.

"I'm sorry, Sage," I said. "What did you say?"

"I said, how can I read my novel in front of the whole school if everyone thinks it is a comedy? George, *Angelica and the Seminole Indians* wasn't meant to be a laughing matter. It's a historical romance. A *romance,* George. How could the English department have been confused by what I wrote?"

Sage kicked through slush as we headed home. "Whoever Anonymous is, they deserve to be the solo winner."

Her eyes were so huge with sadness that I thought I might start bawling, too.

"Maybe I can help you, Sage," I said. "Maybe I can help you straighten tomorrow's chapter out."

Sage glanced at me. "Oh, George, do you think so? Do you think you could fix it?"

"No!" I wanted to shout out. "Nothing but throwing it into the fireplace can fix it." But I didn't say anything. Instead, I bit my lip and stared hard at the road.

"Yeah, I'll help Angelica." I had to. Guilt would make me.

Because to top everything off, I was the anonymous heel who had tied with Sage in the Schoolcraft High School Creative Writing Contest.

27

your eyes, green like the morning sea
make me wonder
if our children's eyes
will smile,
will see things,
will laugh at life,
will cry
the way your eyes do

28
Sage

GEORGE STAYED WITH ME UNTIL LATE THAT EVE-
ning. We sat at the computer in Mom's office, not even
going into the dining room for dinner.

The walls in this room, except for one that was
all windows, were lined with books. Medical books,
the classics, poetry, biographies, and autobiogra-
phies. And of course, all the books Mom has had published.

There were the things I'd grown up with, too: *Anne
of Green Gables,* Dr. Seuss, the Newbery winners. Books
were everywhere.

It made me sad to see them that evening. How many
times had I come in this room and imagined a series of
Angelicas lining one wall? Now I realized what a ridiculous idea that had been.

As George and I went through the first chapter, one
paragraph at a time, I realized how terribly *Angelica* was
written. I felt ashamed. My face was so red, my head
pounded.

Finally, in desperation, I gave up.

"I can't do this," I cried out. "It's too hard. There are

too many problems." I jumped up and went and stood at the window, peering out into the darkness.

Snow fell. It lay thick and unmarked in the side yard. Like icing, it covered the mountain ash, willows, and oak trees. Beyond the trees was our lake. I knew that the mist was rising now, mingling with the snowflakes as they fell into the warmer water. If I hadn't been so brokenhearted, my side yard would have made a perfect Angelica scene. With ravishing Indians and a wild bear or two. Or maybe even a futuristic Cherilena.

George came and stood beside me. He put his arm around my shoulders. I leaned against him. I could see us both in the reflection of the glass. It felt good to stand there so close to him. Even with tomorrow looming ahead.

"Look," George said. "The English staff picked Angelica as a first-place winner out of all the submissions. This is the way they thought you meant for her to be. And Sage, if you look at it that way, you have a funny book here."

"But, George," I said. "I can't read the book and know people are laughing at it. It would be too painful."

George smiled and took my hand. "What would Angelica do?" he asked, and led me back to Mom's chair.

I sat down at the mahogany desk, where I had worked for so many hours. I thought about Angelica, who was almost as real to me as George. What *would* she do?

"She would stand bravely in front of the microphone . . ."

"Her one-eyed lover listening in the crowd . . ."

"And read what she had written," I finished.

George nodded. For the first time since I had heard that I was a Schoolcraft first-place winner, I smiled.

"Right," George said. Or maybe he meant *write*. I couldn't help imagining him in an eye patch.

29

George

T UESDAY SEEMED TO LOOM EVEN DARKER than Monday had. Sure, the business with Ms. Chapin had been scarier than heck, but there were worse things. I could see that now.

First of all, Sage's reading, right after morning announcements. And the fear of meeting up with Boob Taylor again.

Sage and I had worked the whole evening before on her presentation so she could make ridiculous parts seem even more ridiculous, and funny parts even funnier. But she was still scared. And I was afraid for her. Although Sage is dramatic, she's usually only dramatic with me. This would be hard for her.

"Swear you'll stay with me while I'm reading," she said when I opened the door of the school for her.

"Isn't your mom coming?"

"She told me she'd sit in my first-period class, in my chair, with her fingers and toes crossed."

That sounded like something Mrs. Oliver would do. I hoped to goodness she didn't wear a costume.

"So swear you'll stay with me."

"I swear," I said. "I've already sworn. Don't you trust

me?" I felt a pang of guilt asking her that. I mean, I *had* hidden Angelica, and *had* left Sage when the announcements were made about the winner of the contest. Of course she didn't know that, but it didn't ease my guilt any. I *should* have been there for her. That's what Angelica heroes were for.

Poor Sage was so scared her bottom lip trembled. We walked hand in hand down the corridor, then stood close together in the office where Sage met Ms. Chapin.

"Sage Oliver," she said, and smiled. I don't think I've ever seen Ms. Chapin smile, and I've worked with her forever. For a moment I thought she might even hug Sage. But she didn't. Ms. Chapin rested her hand on Sage's shoulder.

"Your book is a riot," she said. "I haven't read anything that funny in years."

"Thank you. I'm glad you like it." Sage sounded humble. Little did Ms. Chapin know just how humble my best friend was.

"I'll read with you," Ms. Chapin said. "No one came forward to claim the collection of poetry, *From My Heart.* I hope someone does soon. I hate speaking over this intercom."

There weren't many announcements that morning. Sage squeezed my hand. She had already let Ms. Chapin know I was there for moral support. The countdown was on.

I closed my eyes when Ms. Chapin read my first poem to the whole school:

> You
> dance close to me
> leading during the songs
> I hear in my head

when I am with
you.

I mouthed the words with her.

Ms. Chapin's smooth voice painted a picture of Sage and me dancing beneath a ballroom chandelier. It was a slow dance. A nice, slow dance. She was a boring teacher, but she sure could read poetry and make it come alive. I wondered if maybe she wrote poetry herself. When I opened my eyes, Sage was staring at me.

"It's you, George," she said, her voice seeming to echo, it was so loud.

"What?" I asked, caught.

"You're the anonymous winner. *You* wrote these poems."

I nodded.

"George Blandford," Ms. Chapin said. "And to think you let me read for you."

"It was a love poem." Sage sounded surprised.

I shrugged. "I wrote it for you, Sage. I wrote them all for you."

Sage threw her arms around my neck. "What? Oh, George, I can't believe it."

"It's true," I said into her hair.

"Thank you," she said, her voice soft.

"The microphone is on," Ms. Chapin said. "Your audience awaits you, Ms. Oliver."

The microphone? Oh, great. So that's why Sage's voice had seemed so loud and echo-y before. It had been. My secret was out.

Sage started to say more, but Ms. Chapin gestured for her while announcing Sage as a wonderful and gifted writer.

"And," Ms. Chapin continued, "now that our mystery contributor has appeared, we'll be letting him do his own reading. Won't we, Mr. Blandford?"

Sage looked back at me. "I can't believe you write such beautiful poetry," she said, and her voice boomed out in the hall.

I shrugged again, and Ms. Chapin nodded at Sage. I smiled my encouragement, then stood behind Sage, my hand on her shoulder. She was warm beneath her sweater.

Sage took a deep breath, and I closed my eyes again. This time I did it in support of her.

And she did okay. She stumbled around at first, then got control of her nerves and read without one mistake. In the front part of the office, I could hear people laughing. Sage was a success.

"You scoundrel," Sage said as we headed back to class. "I can't believe that all those times I wondered who had tied with me, you didn't tell me it was you." She laughed out loud. "It's so wonderful, George."

"I didn't want anyone to know. That's why I submitted it anonymously. A guy writing love poems. It's not cool."

"It is to me," Sage said. And I could see in her eyes that she meant it.

In the hall between classes, whenever I was with Sage, people called out her name and came up to tell her they loved Angelica. Mostly it was girls, which was fine by me.

I stood next to Sage while people congratulated her, or told her they really hated sappy romances but Sage's was pretty funny. A few people never saw the mistakes in the novel, and that was okay, too. Overall, Sage and Angelica got good reviews. And the girls liked my poems, too. Lots of them said they hoped their boyfriends would write stuff like that for them.

"I wish it hadn't turned out this way," Sage said between classes. "I wish this novel was as good as I thought it was. I wish it was as nice as what you've done."

"Nothing really is as good as we think it is, is it?" I asked her. I felt full of wisdom. And realized, for the first time, that I liked Sage's popularity. Not for myself, but for her. I mean, I stood right next to her. What more could I want?

Okay, there was more.

"Why, George Blandford," Sage said. She turned and looked me full in the face. "What a sad way to go through life, thinking you never have the best. Whenever I'm with you, I can't think of a happier time. And I don't wish for a different one, either."

I felt stunned.

The bell rang, and the hall began to clear as a few stragglers rushed around, late, to their classes.

I leaned toward Sage. She gazed up at me, her green eyes even greener because of what she wore.

This is it, I thought. *I'm going to kiss her. I am going to kiss Sage Oliver right here in the halls of Schoolcraft High School.* Right then I felt a strong alliance to my school and its colors.

Sage closed her eyes.

"Blandford," boomed a voice. "Mr. Poet Man." At the end of the hall stood Boob Taylor and a group of his football-player friends.

30
Sage

IT WAS LIKE A WESTERN GUNFIGHT.

At first George leaned down to kiss me.

I was still surprised at the thought that the man of my dreams was a romantic poet. I had just closed my eyes and tilted my head up at George when I heard Bob Taylor.

For a brief moment, I thought of Cherilena and how this would make a great scene in my newest novel. Then I saw all of Bob's friends with him.

The few people still in the hall stopped to watch. George looked at me, sighed, then turned almost in slow motion. His eyes narrowed, and his lips drew into a thin line. I stepped up beside him.

"Hiding behind your prude of a girlfriend?" Bob said.

I suddenly felt steaming mad. George laughed. I couldn't believe it. He laughed.

"I'm not a prude," I said to George.

He smiled. "I know that," he said. I could tell that George was nervous, but he didn't turn from Bob or even flinch when the circle of people gathered around us.

"Only a wuss would hide behind his girlfriend," one of the football players said. "Or a poet." The group of guys mumbled in agreement.

I felt my back stiffen.

"I'm not a fighter," George said. "Anyone in the school could see I'm no match for you, Boob."

"What?" Bob asked, and his voice stretched out.

"Slip of the tongue," George said. "Oops. I mean Bob. *B-o-b*. Not Boob, *b-o-o-b*."

Bob glanced around the circle. No one moved.

George kept talking. "I would be a fool to fight you. So I have to decide what to do. I choose not to fight."

Bob laughed, and the sound was ugly.

"Running, wuss? Running or hiding. That's your way, Blandford, isn't it?" Bob asked, only it wasn't a question.

"All muscle, no brain. That's your way, Taylor, isn't it?" I said, mimicking his tone. A few kids in the circle laughed.

"Don't waste your breath, Sage," George said. "Let's go." He took me by the arm and started to lead me out of the circle, but each way he tried to push past closed tight.

"Let us out of here," I said.

"Hiding again?" Bob asked. He pushed up close to George. George looked right at Bob.

"George," I said. "I don't want you to do this. I want to go to class. We're all going to be late for class."

"This has nothing to do with you, Sage, Famous Romance Writer," Bob said.

I couldn't help it. I still hurt about Angelica. I gasped.

George glanced at me. He saw my face and hit Bob once in the stomach and then in the jaw. The punches caught Bob off guard, and he fell backward.

"Leave her alone," George said, hovering over Bob, his fists still clenched.

Bob jumped to his feet, swearing. "That's it," he yelled. As he rushed up to meet George, I stepped in between them. Bob tried to push me aside.

"Go away, Bob," I shouted. "Leave us alone."

"Move, Sage," George said. "I gotta do this. He's hurt your feelings."

"Yes, Sage," said Bob. "Let him fight me. Let him protect you. Then maybe he can write a poem for you when it's all over. If there's anything left of him." His voice was a sneer.

"I don't need you to protect me, George," I said. I turned until I faced him. Well, I sort of faced him. My chin dug into his chest. It was hard to talk that way, so I pushed back against Bob, who towered over me and even looked down at George. Mashed between them, I felt ridiculous. This was a dangerous place to be. But I couldn't leave George to fight Bob. George had spoken the truth. He would be beaten to a pulp, especially since he had humiliated Bob in front of everyone. "My feelings are no big deal, George. It's okay. I want to go."

"No, Sage, it is not okay." I couldn't believe how angry George was. And all for me. What a great scene this would be for my book. Except the part about being squished between two people. I couldn't quite see Cherilena doing that.

"I am going to put him out of his misery, Sage," Bob said. "If you move out of the way."

142

I turned until my face squished against Bob's chest. I pushed back and looked up at him. The late bell rang.

"We've got to go to class," I said. "Please, Bob, let this go."

"We sure wouldn't want you to be late to class, now, would we, Sage?" He didn't even look at me.

Yuck. I couldn't believe I had actually dated Bob. Why hadn't I noticed his have-to-win attitude before now?

I turned back to George.

"We don't believe in fighting," I said.

"But, Sage," George said. "You slapped him on Friday."

A few murmurs came from the circle of people. I could tell that Bob had left that part of the story out when he talked to his football-player friends.

"I hit him because he was being mean to you, George."

"How sweet," Bob said. Bob pushed me to the side and pressed his face close to George's. "You're not even worthy of my time, Blandford. I have better things to do than wait for your girlfriend to move so I can slug you." He turned then and left, knocking people aside as the circle opened up for him to leave.

"That hurt my hand," George said when we stood alone in the hall. He looked at his knuckles. "I'll never be the hero you want, Sage. I'm not a fighter. I'm a user of words."

"That's exactly what I want, George," I said.

We walked to English. Outside the classroom, George stopped.

"Stand up straight, Sage," he said. "Your public awaits you." Then he opened the door for me.

I smiled, and elbowed George in the side. He grinned.

"And so does yours," I said.

We went into class together.

31
George

WHEN I GOT HOME FROM SCHOOL MOM met me at the door with a message to call Harold Donaldson.

"Hey, Blandford," Mr. Donaldson said, when I got him on the phone. "I've got a copy of your article here. You did a good job. We need someone on the staff to pick up a roving high-school sports position. Interested?"

"Yes," I said. "Yes, you bet." I couldn't believe it. My day was getting better and better. To top it all off, I had Andrew's twenty dollars in my pocket and a date with Sage that evening.

Sage's father drove her to my house at seven o'clock to pick me up. Morgan wasn't with her. We were going to T.G.I. Friday's for dinner. Sage told me that since I'd won the writing contest, too, I was the natural pick to go with her. We were saving my winning coupons for later.

"Are you sure?" I had asked. We were standing outside the newsroom when she told me this. Andrew and Cheri were behind the closed doors doing who-knows-what.

"George, how can you even ask me if I'm sure? Who else would I take with me if you didn't go?"

"This school is crawling with guys that would love to go with you," I said.

"Not Bob Taylor," Sage said. "He's just crawling."

I laughed. Boob had refused to look at Sage in any of the classes they shared, she told me, but he'd made enough comments that he'd finally been asked to leave U.S. history.

Sage looked me right in the eye.

"George, I want to be with you. Not with Bob Taylor. Not with any of the other guys here at Schoolcraft. Not even with any of Angelica's one-eyed lovers."

"What about Cherilena's one-eyed lovers?"

Sage grinned. "Only you," she said. "I've felt this way since second grade."

"Since that day you kissed me?"

"I did not kiss you then. You've imagined that forever. Probably since before you even met me you've imagined it."

I laughed. "Okay, Sage. What time are we going?"

At seven-thirty we were waiting to be served. Jimmy Buffett sang in the background, something about a volcano. It felt great to sit at dinner with Sage and not worry about Angelica. It felt great to know that she wanted to be with me.

I smiled and reached across the table to hold her hand. The candle that sat in a tiny glass cup flickered.

Sage smiled, and it nearly took my breath away. She was so beautiful, her curly hair a halo around her face in a wild rush of reddish blond color, her dress matching her eyes, the string of pearls around her throat. Her perfect lips.

I looked away from Sage and swallowed. There *was* something to worry about. The end of the evening. The end-of-the-evening kiss. Would it come too soon? Would it never get here?

"George," Sage said. "I have an announcement to make."

"You've decided to write the sequel to *Angelica and the Seminole Indians*," I joked.

"Yes," Sage said. "I have decided to do that, after you and I work on this novel, and after Cherilena. But that's not the announcement I have." She cleared her throat, then closed her eyes.

"I'm going to college with you. I mean, I'm planning on trying to get accepted into Kalamazoo Valley Community College."

"You're kidding!" I said. "I cannot believe it. I thought you were through with school as soon as we finished here."

"Well." With her free hand Sage picked up the water glass and drank from it. The candle sparkle reflected in her eyes and on the glass she held. "I'm not so sure school is for me. But I am determined to become a successful writer, George. I have to. I love creating worlds and experiences and lives more than just about anything. I know Angelica wasn't that great. But I can't leave her on the plains, George. I want to make her live as sure as you and I are living. I want people to love her."

I nodded. I knew exactly what Sage meant.

After dinner Sage's dad picked us up.

"Your limo awaits the young couple," he said, opening the back door for us to slide in. "Anyone care for a drive?"

"Yes, Daddy," Sage said. "That would be wonderful."

We took a slow drive from Portage to Centerville so we could go over the old Countervail covered bridge. Bare mountain ash and maples lined the road. An occasional blue spruce sat dark on the white snow. The moon shone full in an almost purple night sky. It illuminated the snow.

Houses were dressed for Christmas, each boasting tiny lights that twinkled off and on.

We drove on to Sage's house.

"I'll walk you home, George," she said.

I got out of the car, and she linked her arm into mine.

I wanted to walk slowly, so slowly the night would not end. I wanted this moment to keep on going, the way Angelica did, never-ending.

At my house, a few lights winked through the windows at us. Our Christmas tree peeked out. Dad had decorated it.

The snow gleamed a bluish color, reflecting the moon. A soft white blanket covered everything, even the sound of our footsteps, as Sage walked me up to the door.

"There's your mother," I said, and gestured with my free hand. Sage turned to look.

Across the backyards that separated our houses, Sage's mother sat on a horse. She rode sidesaddle and wore a long cape. Dr. Oliver led the horse through the knee-deep snow.

"I guess Mom is experimenting again," Sage said. "Another Oliver novel is about to be born."

"My parents are waiting in the living room," I said. "Mom told me she'd make us hot chocolate when we came in." I said all this as I pulled Sage close.

Her breath blew out white. A few strands of wild hair hung down into her face. I pushed them back off her forehead. Her body was bulky against mine because of her coat. She looked up, smiling.

And after what seemed an eternity, I kissed Sage Oliver, the love of my life.

32
Sage

Cherilena looked at her lifelong friend. He stood a head taller than she, and he was longingly gazing down into her eyes. In the background, the half-horse half-woman whinnied her way across the blood-red space snow.

As their lips pressed firmly together, Cherilena's head whirled with happiness. Never had she known such complete bliss as she was experiencing in that very kiss. In her mind, the sun blazed, stars danced, water gurgled, the earth moved.

"Wow," Cherilena cooed. "It was worth the wait. My first kiss with you, Man-I-Have-Been-Waiting-For." She was breathless.

"That's our second kiss," he complained.

"No, our first," she giggled. She looked ever so closely at her man. Yes, even after the kiss he was still as handsome as ever to her.

His brown eyes, one hidden behind an eye patch, smiled at her. Her green eyes smiled back.